MIDAIR

ALSO BY KODI SCHEER

Incendiary Girls

KODI SCHEER

MIDAIR

Published by Little A, New York

www.apub.com

Amazon, the Amazon logo, and Little A are trademarks of Amazon.com, Inc., or its affiliates.

ISBN-10 (hardcover): 1503934128
ISBN-13 (hardcover): 9781503934122

ISBN-10 (paperback): 1503934101
ISBN-13 (paperback): 9781503934108

Cover design by Shasti O'Leary Soudant

Printed in the United States of America

for the Lunch Bunch

A swimmer in distress cries, "I shall drown; no one will save me!" A suicide puts it the other way: "I will drown; no one shall save me!"

—William Strunk Jr. and E. B. White

I had a secret: I wanted to leave the earth in a spectacular fashion. Specifically, by leaping from the Eiffel Tower. The end seemed ideal—high above the city, soaring through the air just as my heart stopped and my brain released a rush of endorphins, causing intense euphoria. A moth consumed by the light.

Best of all, I'd get to see Vince again, and not just in the occasional dream. Vincent: my brother, my voice, my world. My world had abruptly ended the previous year, when Vince died, collapsing during practice the day before he was to compete in the 1,600-meter relay at the state track meet.

I was one step closer to my goal, an hour or so from landing at de Gaulle. I didn't want to think about the giant aluminum bird hurling through the sky or how we were all at the mercy of fate and engineering. Sweat prickled under my arms. A plane disaster would completely ruin my plans. I wanted oblivion, but on my own terms. I gulped the last of my mini bottle of red wine and repeated a mantra: *please don't crash*.

My travel companions were still asleep. They were newly minted high school graduates, the class of 1999, liberated from childhood and poised for the new millennium. Whitney, Kiran, and Kat were ready for adventure in the most romantic city in the world. More than acquaintances, but certainly not my friends, they were generally pleasant, at least to my face.

We'd been thrown together by circumstance in Madame Davis's French classes at Washington High School, located in a western suburb of Chicago far enough from the city to be the commuter train's last stop. I'd gone to Prairie High, a small, rural school that only offered Spanish, so I drove a half hour each way to both escape Prairie and learn a more glamorous language. Madame Davis usually led a trip to France every other summer, but she'd recently announced her retirement. We were the only ones willing to raise funds (which we did by soliciting local businesses) and go it alone.

The girls seemed ready to slice open the oyster of the world and suck its flesh from the shell. Poor things, they had such high expectations. Take Kiran, the type of girl people in my small town would describe as "exotic," her flawless brown skin accentuated by her muted gray University of Michigan T-shirt and jeans. Though petite, she was a varsity athlete in both track and swimming. At O'Hare, she'd announced she was "so psyched" for Paris. She was always optimistic and upbeat. And too damn naïve.

Whitney was an all-American cliché, with straight, bleached teeth and natural blonde hair. She looked like an ad for wholesome dairy products. She was also an emotional roller coaster. I could never tell when she was on her way up, but the descent was obvious and usually ended in waterworks. When the Chase branch manager had promised a donation for our trip but didn't come through, she had bawled like a child. I had no sympathy for someone who lacked such control. Oh no, the other cheerleaders won't talk to me! It's, like, totally worse than Y2K!

Finally, there was Kat, who so resembled Uma Thurman in *Pulp Fiction* that people often looked twice—not only did she sport the raven bob with a fringe of square-cut bangs, vermillion lips, and heavy eyeliner, but she actually wore crisp white shirts with black pants. She was smart enough to be cynical yet had nothing to be cynical *about*. Her parents had graduate degrees, they lived in a house with more bedrooms than people, and her first car was a BMW coupe. Kat also had sex with anything that moved. But her most heinous crime was cheating off my ACTs.

I used to believe that if I worked hard and ignored the vortex of my small-town high school, I'd be rewarded in college. Perseverance, and lots of patience, would be my ticket. I'd been the quiet, bookish girl at Prairie, where it was a crime to be smart. I clung to the hope of college like a life raft, and along with my brother Vince, that hope kept me afloat for years. Then Vince died. Still, I studied hard and aced the ACT—scoring a perfect 36. And the ACT regulators somehow concluded that *I'd* cheated. Suddenly, the life raft capsized, sending me into the murky abyss. All I could see was darkness.

Soon Kat would watch me jump from the world's most iconic monument, but before I did, I'd tell her exactly why: she'd ruined my life. The final nail in my coffin. My blood would be on her hands—I would haunt her until the day she died. My plan was beautiful in its simplicity.

I turned to observe the girls I'd spend my last days with. Kiran, the ingénue, was sitting next to me, her head tilted back and eyes twitching in sleep. I peered over the seats to gaze at Whitney, the emotional crier, her eyes crusted shut, and Kat, whose mouth lolled open with glistening saliva, ready for the giant dick of reality.

I wanted to shake each of them and say, *wake up!*

In truth, I envied my travel companions having so many possibilities for a bright future, accented by this sophisticated European adventure. They wanted to know how high the Arc de Triomphe appeared from the Champs-Élysées and how French women practiced the art of seduction. What did a fresh Parisian baguette taste like? What color were the Tuileries in June? How many twinkling lights illuminated the Eiffel Tower at dusk?

My companions had simple needs. They each wanted to fuck a chain-smoking French guy in an alley that smelled of croissants and lust. They wanted to buy black stilettos and learn to strut thirty blocks in them. They wanted to order an extravagant meal, maybe even escargot, with lots of champagne.

I imagined how each girl began the day. Kat probably rose to find an empty house, her mother on a dig in Syria and her father at a legal conference. She fed their English bulldog his special kibble that prevented digestive issues before sitting outside on the patio in her red kimono. She enjoyed a Marlboro Light and espresso, vowing to smoke only French cigarettes while in Paris. Her mother had left a note with the combo to the fireproof lockbox, where

Kat could find her passport. She called the airport limo service to double-check their arrival time.

Whitney awoke to the smell of pancakes (and later discovered they were actually crêpes) because her father was preparing an extravagant farewell breakfast. Her older sister, Ashley, on break from U of I and yet to start her internship with a physical therapy clinic, joined the party by wearing a black beret and fake mustache. Ashley got strawberry compote on the mustache, which gave all of them a good laugh. Whitney promised to take lots of pictures and send postcards.

In Kiran's house, her mother made scrambled eggs with green peppers, which Kiran liberally doused with hot sauce. Her father, back from the night shift at the ER, did the same and asked if there was any leftover roti or naan from the evening meal. Her younger sister, Sarita, had test prep books and notes strewn across the Formica table, which their mother insisted must be put away at once. Kiran put a star on the fridge calendar to remind them of her return flight.

All three of my travel companions looked over what they'd packed and hoped they weren't forgetting anything. Their stomachs felt just a touch queasy, which they chalked up to excitement. While we were all sitting in the international terminal at O'Hare, they accepted my offer of spearmint gum. That's the smell I remember, mint, along with stale hairspray and the faintest whiff of female perspiration.

Of course that trip haunts me. I regret what I did—I was young and myopic. But that's no excuse. My dark, twisted soul exuded dark, twisted logic. Would I take it back? Yes. A thousand times yes. Would I trade places with her? Depends on the day. It's been almost seventeen years. But today, *oui*. Without a doubt. I deserved her fate.

Because I had the brilliant (if misguided) idea to christen my daughter after her, I say or write her name often, cheering her on at soccer matches and swim meets and writing her name on field trip permission slips. Perhaps it's a defense mechanism, but I usually call my daughter by her nickname, Cricket. She was born with a full head of black hair and a quiet cry that punctuated the night.

I hope, desperately, that she never becomes the girl I once was.

The dimmed cabin lights couldn't hide the other girls' vulner-ability. I had the urge to pinch Whitney's nostrils or even poke a finger in Kat's gaping mouth. She was drooling, for Christ's sake. It was an overnight flight, and everyone else was sleeping while I stewed, kept awake by my overactive imagination. I was impatient to be in the City of Light. Amused by the romantic moniker of Paris, especially given my dark plan, I flipped through the bilingual airline magazine and ended up filling in all the crossword squares with my pen. I scribbled so hard that the tip of my pen broke through the paper.

At some point, the cabin lights brightened and I heard clatter-ing food carts. The chic flight attendant handed everyone breakfast trays with cold, flour-dusted rolls and sad grapes shrouded in plas-tic. Beside me, Kiran started to wake up. The groggy anesthesia of sleep began to wear off, turning to recognition.

I looked over the seats behind us. Whitney was still asleep, her head resting on her left shoulder, with no audible snoring. Kat had woken up and was brushing the collar of her white shirt where she'd slobbered. But no amount of fussing would dry the wet spot. She also had smudges of mascara under her eyes, smeared lines of charcoal from each lash. Kat took a compact mirror from her purse and must've seen the damage. Rather than correct it, she put on a pair of large black sunglasses.

"Bonjour!" said Kiran, not waiting for my answer. She twisted around to greet Kat and Whitney. *"Bonjour, mes amies!"*

"Hey," Whitney said, rubbing the crust from the corners of her eyes.

"You must be one of those *morning* people," said Kat.

I wanted to correct her: it would be 9:00 a.m. Paris time, but only 2:00 a.m. Central Standard Time—perfect for a night owl. She was such a poseur.

"What's with the shades?" asked Whitney. She was finger-combing her long golden mane.

"My eyes are sensitive," Kat snapped.

"Whatever," said Whitney, who stopped combing to make a "W" sign with her fingers. "You just want to look all mysterious."

"Guess what?" Kiran said. "We're almost in Paris! I bet we're in French airspace."

I felt the pressure building in my ears and unwrapped a stick of gum. The captain's disembodied voice informed us of the initial descent and reminded us to buckle our seat belts, which were like the lap restraints on carnival rides. I'd expected them to be more like car seat belts, like the ones in my mom's rusted Escort where the strap went over your chest as well as your lap.

When we'd taken the car to pick up my brother Vince's ashes—a burial had been too expensive—I insisted that we put the gray marble urn in the front seat and buckle him in. As kids, we'd always fought about who got shotgun.

That meant my mother had to sit in back, but she was out of it, drugged up on sedatives that I suspected she'd filched from the nursing home her first shift after Vince died. The coroner said cardiac issues in healthy young athletes were rare but did occur, which gave us little comfort. I hated the thought of his heart being sliced open by a stranger in a surgical mask. He'd had an aortic aneurysm—the walls of his heart were too weak.

We'd agreed to spread some of his ashes at his favorite place: Werners' pond. Vince and I used to ride our bikes out here as kids and swim on our backs, calling out the shapes we saw in the clouds. Or we'd jump from the tire swing, Vince pushing me so hard that I reached the middle of the pond before letting myself fall in.

I unscrewed the top of the urn, my hands damp with anxiety. I scooped the gray, silty remains with my fingertips. The fragments of bone were the easiest to toss into the water.

"Good-bye, Vincent," said our mother, throwing a handful of her son, my brother, in powdered form, into Werners' pond. "Wish your father was here."

"Really?" I asked. When I was ten years old, my father, a freight conductor, had hopped the Burlington Northern and never returned.

"You're probably right," my mother replied.

Though it'd only been two weeks, she'd aged ten years since Vince died. I finally saw her for who she truly was: a grieving forty-year-old woman with a face slack as a washcloth. She'd dreamed of being a pediatrician, but married young and had two kids, then settled for being a nurse's aide. The residents at the Pine Haven Nursing Home loved her. They lived in the past, just as my mother did now, with her favorite child.

I was so angry at my mother for having an obvious favorite. In some ways, I couldn't blame her. He was everyone's favorite: affectionate, charming, and always telling you exactly what you needed to hear. I was standoffish and never had the right words. Sometimes I found them, but long after the fact.

So losing me would be nothing compared to losing Vince. Still, I was considerate enough to off myself in Paris so my mother would never have to find the body.

When I'd reached into the urn, some of the ash had stuck to my sweaty fingers. What could I do? This was my brother, and it seemed disrespectful to wipe him on the seat of the Escort or wash him down the drain. So I licked my index finger, gagging on the taste of rotten eggs and sand. I was both repulsed and compelled to lick the rest of my fingers, swallowing the ash and clinging to the memory of my brother.

He'd never been on a plane, either. Now my ears felt like they were going to explode, so I added another piece of gum and chewed harder. Kiran had been kind enough to give me the window seat (and couldn't believe that I'd never flown before). I gripped the armrests. I knew that, statistically, the most dangerous times were during takeoff and landing. *Don't crash and ruin my plans,* I thought.

From this height, France looked exactly like the Midwest—neat squares of green, cut like lime Jell-O salad from the nursing home cafeteria. Yet when the wheels finally hit the tarmac, I wanted to clap, to make sound from my lurching, twisted joy. We hadn't crashed. I was still in full control.

O ur first hours in Paris were spent in the line for immigration and then customs.

"This is ridiculous," Kat said, and blew on her fringe of black bangs. "Fucking French inefficiency. Three international flights come in at the same time, and suddenly it's like the bread lines in Moscow."

As if Kat knew true hardship.

"I, like, expect better in a first-world country," said Whitney. She had the most luggage, and each bag was monogrammed with her initials. Her sister or father or someone who cared for her had taken the trouble to tie bright-red yarn bows around the handles, presumably so she could spot them on the baggage carousel. There was no way that Whitney had come up with that idea on her own.

She was struggling to corral all of her bags each time we rounded a barricade in the never-ending line. I probably should've helped Whitney, as I'd packed light, only a messenger bag. It wasn't as though I'd need much for the next few days, and I wouldn't be returning home.

"No offense, Kiran," Kat added. I assumed she was referring to the notion that India was part of the so-called Third World.

"None taken," Kiran chirped. She had the most international travel experience of any of us, having family in Punjab. But she insisted that India didn't really count. She also insisted that we pronounce her name like the Irish version—KEER-uhn—rather than use the pronunciation of her parents' native dialect.

"Was India a total shithole?" I asked, even though I knew the answer. She hated when anyone drew attention to her parents' birthplace.

"Most definitely," she replied. "Never go there."

"Amazing food plus the Taj Mahal?" said Kat. "Seems interesting to me." She had propped her sunglasses on her head like a tiara. The mascara smudges were gone.

"Yeah, I guess it's interesting," Kiran said. "If you like malaria and rabid monkeys."

"You had malaria?" Whitney asked. "No freaking way. Who'd you get it from?"

I couldn't let this one go. "It's a mosquito-borne infection."

"It was horrible," Kiran said. Her right arm was extended straight, holding her elbow with the opposite hand, stretching her shoulder. She often used downtime to stretch, probably because she was always running and swimming.

"Is it like AIDS, where you have the virus all the time?" Whitney asked.

"Nah. The meds cure it." Kiran bent into a squat and as she stood up, arched her back. The block "M," for the University of Michigan, stretched across her chest. I didn't understand why she was wearing a Michigan T-shirt when she was headed to the University of Chicago in the fall.

Her boobs were bigger than mine, though not by much—maybe hers were a small B-cup. I was skinny and flat-chested and hadn't gotten my period until I was fifteen. I kept a running inventory of everyone's breast size—not because I had any sexual interest, but because I longed to have breasts of my own, and I couldn't help but notice what they had and I didn't. I was a pauper who noted every sign of wealth. Whitney had to be a generous C-cup, and Kat wore a 32D. I knew the specifics because we'd had a French Club meeting at her McMansion, and in her bathroom suite, I'd seen a day's worth of dirty laundry on the floor, including a lacy Victoria's Secret bra with the tag sticking out.

Sometimes I sized up strangers, like the twentysomething brunette in line ahead of us who was fanning herself with her Canadian passport. The ideal size, not too big or too small—probably 32C.

We kept meeting the same people in line, separated only by the cloth tape that ran from post to post. A tall guy our age with acne and spiked hair and wearing all black was blasting music from his Discman so loud that we could hear it through the headphones. He looked more Scandinavian or German than French.

"That song," Whitney said. "I heard it like twice on the plane."

It had a catchy dance beat. But I couldn't make out the lyrics.

"Me, too," said Kiran. "What's it saying? *I'm blue, I will bleed, I will die?*"

"It's just nonsense," Kat announced. "Like that 'Da Da Da' song on the Volkswagen commercial."

"But it really does sound like *'I'm blue, I will bleed, I will die,'*" said Whitney.

I was amused—it was perfect. I'd soon bleed and die, but my heart would stop first. Just as my brother's had.

"Hey," Kat said, tugging on the guy's shirtsleeve. "What's that song?"

He took off the headphones. They made a horseshoe around his neck. *"Vhut?"*

"The music," Kat said, louder and with more enunciation, as though he were deaf. Then she pointed to his ear. "What is the MUSICAL SONG?"

"Yes," he replied. "Eiffel 65. The song is 'Blue.'"

Eiffel 65? Another sign that my plan had merit. *Sometimes,* I thought, *the world was just.*

"Is that a boy band?" asked Whitney, twirling a lock of blonde hair in a coquettish way. "Like *NSYNC or Backstreet Boys?"

I didn't think he understood the question until he wrinkled his nose. "No, no, from Italy."

Then he smiled. "You like cigars just as your president?"

"Eww, you perv," Kat said, and repeated it using both syllables. "Per-vert. President Clinton rules the free world. What has yours done lately?"

He shrugged and put the headphones back on. I still didn't know his nationality—maybe Eastern European? We inched forward in line.

"Why would the president put a cigar up inside her, anyway?" Kiran asked, referring to Monica Lewinsky's testimony for the Starr Report.

Kat cocked an eyebrow. "So it would *taste* like her."

"Oh."

I hadn't known either, but it wasn't exactly a burning question for me. I remembered overhearing Vince and his friends joking about a girl who tasted like tuna. I'd actually caught Vince once, with his tongue down the throat of cheerleader Kristy Schilling, atop our washing machine. I ducked away, grateful I hadn't seen anything more, and we never spoke of it.

Yet I'd had a crush on Vince's friend Jeremiah "Miah" Cunningham for as long as I could remember, and I imagined him kissing me against the washer. Miah was the only one of Vince's friends to truly acknowledge my presence, asking "How's it going, Nessie?" or sometimes, "What's up, chicken butt?" Of course, I never had a clever reply.

Since Miah had his own car, he often drove Vince around, and when they didn't have practice or Vince wasn't hanging out with some girl, Miah would give me a ride home. Even though it was a five-minute drive (or twenty-minute walk), I wanted those minutes to last forever. Mostly we listened to Nirvana or Pearl Jam. I kept hoping that he'd suddenly recognize my unconventional beauty or intellect. Needless to say, that never happened.

Vince liked to tell me, "Ness, you're going to be really pretty when you're older." He meant it as a compliment, but it hurt all the same.

What I wouldn't give to see Vince again. I'd carried around that damn urn all the time, leaving it on my dresser when I was at school. At night, when our sedative-laced mom was asleep, I'd take it to the Escort, strap it under the passenger seat belt, and drive.

The car didn't have air-conditioning, so I had to roll down the windows and drive fast enough that the bugs didn't get inside. I raced down country roads so empty I could leave my brights on the whole time. Insects flew at the windshield like snow.

I'd scream as loud as I could. Then I'd turn to the passenger seat and yell at Vince: "Why? Why did you leave me here alone? How could you?"

Or some such variation.

Sometimes I'd swear at him, calling him a piece of shit or a fucking bastard. Other times I'd plead, trying to elicit sympathy, telling him about the rash I'd developed under my eyes from crying. Or mentioning that I couldn't eat—not when he could never taste food again. Or saying that our mother was a zombie. All of those things were true. But I always felt just as empty when I pulled back into the driveway.

One night it dawned on me: I could make him proud. He'd constantly called me his genius little sister. He even told strangers that I could get into Harvard. I vowed to my dead brother that not only would I be the first in the family to go to college, I'd get a full ride.

I didn't know anyone who'd attended an Ivy League school. The idea was so foreign to me that I didn't apply to Harvard, a place I'd only heard of from TV or movies, so I set my sights on the University of Illinois. It was the best public school in the state; plus Miah was a freshman there, and I wanted to impress him. I was already top of my (small) high school class, with a 4.0, as well as editor of the yearbook and newspaper. At Prairie, nobody else wanted these positions—the jobs were too much work without much reward. So I'd been given the responsibilities by default.

All I had to do was get a good score on the ACT. I'd studied and had taken multiple practice tests, scoring in the low to mid-30s, within the top percentiles nationally. I convinced myself that I was capable of greatness. Deep down, I had to persuade myself that I was extraordinary in order to keep going, day after day.

A t Charles de Gaulle airport, we got on an escalator enclosed in a plastic tube, one of many tubes traversing the terminal. They looked like the arteries of a giant robot heart.

"This feels like the '70's version of the future," said Kiran.

"For real," echoed Whitney.

We followed the signs to ground transportation, planning to take a cab into the city. But as the automatic doors opened, we found a curious sight: rows of silver Mercedes taxis blocking much of the road. But no one was getting in them. Some of the cabbies were circling on the sidewalk, holding posters I translated as "Equal Pensions NOW!"

"Are you kidding? Seriously?" said Kat. "A strike?"

I scanned the guidebook and offered a suggestion, secretly pleased by another setback for them: "There's a bus."

"I am *not* taking a bus," Whitney said. "Not, like, with all this luggage."

A younger guy in a fitted T-shirt, dark jeans, and sleek black sneakers approached us. "*Mes amies.* You are American?"

"Who wants to know?" demanded Kat.

He put his hands up in surrender and gave a high-voltage movie-star smile. "I like to practice my English is all."

I could already see Kat staking a claim on him.

He introduced himself as Luc.

"Well, Luc," Kat said, a smirk on her crimson lips, "you can practice on me any time."

"You are staying in Paris?" he asked.

We nodded. I couldn't tell if Luc was ignoring the subtext of Kat's reply or was simply oblivious. Whitney flipped her hair in earnest.

"My friend is over there," Luc said, waving at a guy driving a white van wedged between two taxis. His friend waved back, both windows down. Luc explained that their roommate's flight had been cancelled, and since they'd driven their landlord's van, they'd be happy to take us into the city. If we agreed to go to their party tomorrow night.

They seemed interesting enough, but I wasn't convinced that we should spend an entire evening with them. Then again, I could always fake a headache and stay at our rental, drafting my suicide note. I doubted the guys would even notice my absence. I was good at being invisible.

"Well, if they're psychos," whispered Whitney, "at least they're hot. Let's do it."

Kat was all in, and I think Kiran just wanted everyone to be happy. I shrugged, ambivalent. My former crush, Miah, had recently rejected me—I didn't have much hope that any guys would be interested.

Miah had come back for the summer to work as a foreman in his family's contracting business. Emboldened by the fact that I was ending my life, I figured it wouldn't hurt to ask him out. Miah was working on the house down the block, so I brought lemonade and asked, as casually as possible, if he wanted to go to a movie sometime. He laughed. When he realized I was serious, he said, "Nessie, you know you're like a sister to me, right?" So that was that.

Luc led us to the van. The driver hopped out, and they graciously loaded all our luggage.

"And what has brought you Americans to my city?" the friend asked. He was even more handsome, tall but well proportioned, with a Mediterranean complexion and wavy black hair—the ideal figure model for a drawing class.

"*Your* city?" I asked. I refused to be a shrinking violet any longer. What did I have to lose? I could flirt, too. I just didn't really know how.

"Yes, *my* city," he replied haughtily. "I am the king."

He startled me by taking my hand and kissing it. "My lady."

"Your name, King?" asked Kat.

"Anton," he told us, then fixed his green eyes on Kiran.

"Your names are Luc and Anton?" asked Whitney, incredulous. I assumed she'd been expecting more traditional French names.

"Yes," he replied. "Do you not have names?"

We introduced ourselves in order, left to right, and they motioned us into the van.

My travel companions briefly fought over who would sit where. There was only one long bench seat, but the two girls in the center would have better access to the new love interests. I didn't want to waste energy bickering with the girls, so I sat by the window.

Except Luc got in the driver's seat. Anton surprised all of us by squeezing between Kat and Whitney, encouraging Kat to sit up front. I could feel his thigh against mine. I'd never been in such close physical contact with a guy—at least not on purpose. When he turned his radiant attention toward me, it felt as though the sun were illuminating my face in deep winter. I thought of that Camus quote from *The Stranger*, the one on my obtuse guidance counselor's inspirational poster about finding summer amidst winter.

I had ended up reading the quote in context by devouring the entire book. Its protagonist is a sociopath. Life's absurd and then we die. Since death is everyone's end, why delay the inevitable, especially when you had full control?

Yet Anton's attention, his warm hand on my knee, creeping up my leg, planted a seed of doubt. Was I really so weak as to fall for the first guy who'd touched me in an affectionate way? No, of course not. It was just a test. I wasn't like the other girls—I didn't believe in love or affection anymore. It was all self-serving anyway. We die alone.

And why would Anton like me as opposed to the other girls? I was gangly, all collarbones and knees, with barely enough cleavage to fill out my A-cups.

"Vanessa," he said. "You are of the French descent, no? From the south?"

The question threw me. People often assumed that I was something other than just "American," but nobody had ever asked if I was French. My own mother called me "striking," which was a kind way of saying I wasn't ugly, but I wasn't exactly beautiful, either.

I found my voice: *"Non."*

To make sure I wouldn't fall for him, I added, *"J'aime les filles."*

I regretted saying that I liked girls just as the words fell from my mouth. Kiran, who had the best grasp of French, was giving me a weird look.

"Filles uniquement?" he asked. Only girls? And then he leered at Kiran.

"Non," I said, shaking my head, hoping to make it clear that Kiran wasn't a lesbian. *"Pas qu'elle."*

What had I done? I might be safe from his advances, but I was strangely disappointed to lose his attention.

My heritage (and my daughter Cricket's) is nebulous. My great-grandmother was rumored to be of Native American descent—that's why my dad, Vince, and I had olive skin, high cheekbones, and wide-set eyes. Otherwise, we were European mutts, some mix of Irish, German, and English.

My Irish great-grandfather didn't believe in divorce, so he had my perfectly sane great-grandmother committed to a mental hospital, leaving my grandfather without a mother. A husband had the authority to do that in the 1930s. Needless to say, all ties to her side of the family have been lost.

When I was little, I tanned to a deep brown in the summers. On the first day of third grade, Nick Baker called me the n-word. That's how white my small town was—I don't think he actually believed I was black, but he did recognize that I was Other. I said nothing. What was there to say?

Along with my intellect, extreme shyness, and physical awkwardness—a trifecta easily recognized and exploited by my classmates—I was different in appearance. My brother was also swarthy, but Vincent had always fit in where I hadn't. He was gregarious and athletic, while I was introverted and clumsy. Yet when the other kids said I was a Mute Martian or Helen Keller (when they noticed me at all), Vince defended me. I will always be grateful for that.

So I found solace in books. I was a voracious and precocious reader. The heroines who were smart and kind and worked hard were always rewarded in the end, and I was foolish enough to believe that the world worked that way.

But then I started reading more honest literature, such as *The Diary of Anne Frank* and *Hamlet*, and watching foreign films. I memorized the only French VHS movie in my small town's public library—*Breathless*—probably a donation from a well-meaning mom who'd once dreamed of traveling abroad. Almost no one left my town, and the few who did made it as far as suburban Chicago.

I believed *Breathless* to be, in some ways, the French version of *Breakfast at Tiffany's*. Like its American counterpart, it features a glamorous young woman and her seemingly hopeless paramour— but *Breathless* has a darker edge I used to find more believable. Her lover dies, and not in some heroic way, but in a heist gone wrong. People who are bad die. People who are good die. What was the use?

Life is meaningless. At least that's what I thought when I was young. Fortunately, my daughter doesn't think that way. She, too, is a precocious reader. When Cricket read *The Diary of Anne Frank*, she—like the protagonist—still believed in the good of humanity. She wants to see Anne's house in Amsterdam.

But she's been begging to go to Paris for as long as I can remember. I blame those damn *Madeline* books for her initial interest— my husband, not knowing about my ill-fated trip, brought home one of the books. He read it to her that night, the first of countless evenings spent reciting those cutesy rhymes. To this day, I can still recite that book from memory, starting with its opening:

In an old house in Paris
That was covered with vines
Lived twelve little girls
In two straight lines . . .

Luc, who along with his friend Anton saved us from taking the bus into the City of Light, gunned the van as fast as it could go. The highways in France resembled those in the States, except the vehicles were smaller and there was a noticeable absence of SUVs. Plus the van was a stick shift—most of the cars here seemed to be manual.

Kat was sitting shotgun, her right elbow propped on the window, having bummed a smoke from Luc. Whitney was pointing out the handful of billboards, far fewer than on the freeway to O'Hare, and asking Anton and Luc to translate. Our French saviors didn't seem to enjoy that game, because eventually they stopped answering. Kiran was speaking French, inquiring about the taxi strike. Kat and Whitney acted annoyed when they couldn't follow the conversation.

"It's our way," shrugged Luc, still speaking in French. "The Revolution, riots—we like to voice our displeasure in the streets."

"Why are the taxis on strike?" Kiran asked. "Money?"

I assumed she meant wages, but I didn't know the word, either.

Anton sniffed. "Who knows? And who cares? We take the metro."

"Speak English," demanded Kat. "No *comprende*, cowboy."

Through the windshield, I couldn't see anything unique about France, just the flat highway and power lines and green brush beyond the guardrails. But then we started passing tall, corrugated metal barriers. Almost every inch was covered in graffiti, which I couldn't decipher in English, let alone French. I wondered if they were sound barriers for the suburbs or visual barriers for the motorists. Unlike suburban America, I knew, the outlying areas of Paris were populated by immigrants and the working poor. The *banlieues* were basically the projects.

"Yes," said Luc. "English. All American girls are sluts?"

"Is that a *question*?" said Kat.

"Yeah," said Whitney. "That is so unfair."

I was surprised by their defensiveness. They'd seemed so eager to please, but maybe it was a reverse psychology thing. I knew nothing about the art of seduction, but I suspected that they had more experience. It made sense that Anton liked American girls if he thought they were easy to get into bed.

Now we were passing office parks with corporate names I didn't recognize. Some hotels, too, including a Marriott.

"We like to tease," said Anton, squeezing my thigh. "You are all sexy, and to be friends? Exquisite."

This was unprecedented. I didn't know how to react. Was I supposed to squeeze his thigh? Smile and giggle? But then he gripped Kiran's leg. I didn't know if he was hedging his bets, trying to get at least one of us to fall for him, or maybe he was just flirtatious with everyone.

I could tell the other girls had melted, too. Kat was smirking, even with the cigarette glamorously perched at the side of her mouth. Whitney was blushing. And Kiran, the ingénue, was biting her lip. Finally, Kat broke the silence.

"So tell me," she said. "At McDonald's, is the Quarter Pounder really called the Royale with Cheese because of the metric system?"

Both Luc and Anton laughed.

"I knew you are familiar, Uma Thurman," Luc said, bringing his fingers together and kissing them before flicking them outward with gusto. "Mmm. But Tarantino. We import the American culture—we have the Burger King and the advertisement for American film like you will see, *The Mummy*. All over Paris."

The Mummy was a big-budget movie with Brendan Fraser that had been released a month ago, some kind of horror-adventure thing that Vince would've liked. I had no idea it had invaded France, let alone was featured on posters in such a sophisticated city. I was embarrassed on behalf of all Americans.

"It is," Anton said, "like comic book."

I didn't have a clue what he was talking about, but I thought he was referring to the absurdity of American imperialism.

"We say 'MacDo.'" Luc rolled his window down and spit, as if disgusted by the conversation. "And Tarantino, very wrong. We say 'Le Royal Cheese' because the food as measurements—how do you say?—vulgar. We do not say, kiss me with lip for one minute thirty seconds and then kiss with tongue for ninety seconds."

By the time he'd finished, both Luc and Anton were smiling. We were all in love with them. They were gorgeous and smart and French—what wasn't to love?

"What will you see?" asked Anton. "In the city?"

All of the other girls answered at once, in a teenage chorus. "The Louvre! The Musée d'Orsay! The Eiffel Tower!"

And then Luc quashed their dreams, saying that museum workers at the Louvre and the Musée d'Orsay were also on strike for the next two days, at least according to *Le Monde*. He wasn't sure about the Eiffel Tower. I prayed, in my secular way, that the tower would be open, as well as Père Lachaise, the famous (and beautiful) cemetery.

I had to find a way to isolate Kat at *la tour Eiffel* and ensure she was the only one to witness my fate. I wanted Whitney and Kiran to see that the world was ridiculously unfair and experience minor suffering, but I didn't want them to see me jump. I just had to figure out how to make all of this work.

M *erde,"* Luc said, looking down at the instrument panel of the van's dashboard.

Kat laughed. "At least *I'm* not stupid enough to run out of gas."

Yeah, I thought, *but not smart enough to ace a test without cheating.* I sat up straighter to see the fuel gauge, which indicated an empty tank. Luc angled the van toward the next exit, which appeared to have a service station sandwiched between office parks.

We stopped and got out of the van to stretch. Some might call the day sublime, with its big, cottony clouds and the sun warming our faces. It was maybe seventy degrees, ideal for most people, but I didn't believe in ideals anymore. After so much time in cramped spaces, I did appreciate a few minutes outside.

While Anton pumped the gas, I noted the small differences. Gasoline was priced in liters, of course, and there were more pumps for diesel. Kat had to pee, so we all went into the station.

It was disappointingly similar to its American counterparts. Even the items for sale were essentially the same: cigarettes, coffee, chips, and candy bars. Lots of American brands: Lay's, Coca-Cola, and even Halls cough drops. But Kat discovered one major difference: the bathrooms required payment. The lock had a slot for coins, but none of us had any change. Luc had to get a token from the cashier, explaining that it could be used as credit if we wanted to buy anything.

"What?" said Whitney. "You have to pay to go to the bathroom?"

"That is *bullshit*," Kat said. "You should be striking for free bathrooms. That's, like, a human right."

Luc simply shrugged. "You will meet Madame Pipi in Paris. She is the attendant of the toilet and you pay her tip. That is how the French toilets work."

I surveyed the items for sale. The potato chips had different flavors like *fromage* and *moutarde* pickles, which didn't sound particularly appetizing. There were packages of bonbons, fruit candies, and black licorice. Many of the candy bars were nougat or caramel. All of the major newspapers were available: *Le Monde*, *Le Figaro*, and the *International Herald Tribune*. French magazines, too, like *Elle* and *Vogue*.

Despite her indignation, Kat ended up using the token credit for a coffee, which she doused with a liberal amount of cream and sugar. She also got a chocolate bar, sharing the little rectangles of sweet goodness with all of us. *How very generous of her,* I thought bitterly.

Back on the highway, Luc asked us where we were staying. The city spread before us, much flatter and less shiny than most American metropolises, but undeniably more picturesque. The wide boulevards and stone row houses seemed ready-made for postcards.

"We rented an apartment," Kiran replied. "A pied-à-terre on the Île de la Cité."

"*Oh làlà,*" said Anton. Instead of "OOH la LA," which was how we'd say it, Anton said "OH là là," the last two syllables in quick succession.

"It's nice?" asked Whitney.

"Yes, expensive," said Luc. "Many tourists. A big hospital and of course Notre-Dame. We live far, in Belleville."

Luc and Anton began to point out the landmarks visible from the freeway, starting with four skyscrapers, aligned in a square, looking ridiculously out of place amid the nineteenth-century architecture. They comprised the National Library of France, Anton told us.

"On our right," said Luc, "you see the Gare de Lyon train station. To our left, you see le Jardin des Plantes."

The other girls oohed and aahed. I suspected it was partially due to the sights but also in deference to Luc and Anton.

To be fair, I was amazed by the expansive boulevards and neat, uniform rows of stone buildings—the city looked just like the iconic black-and-white photographs. I'd read that in the 1850s, the architect Haussmann was charged with making the city more open and airy, which meant destroying many of the medieval streets and wooden row houses. The elegant Haussmannian buildings, made from the local limestone, were a creamy gray hue in the sunlight. All of them had tall French windows and dark mansard roofs. Most featured a shop or café on the first floor and residential spaces on the second through sixth floors.

The sidewalks were wide and bustling with people: confused tourists with maps, annoyed people with cigarettes, seasoned residents with dogs, and on one corner, an older Parisian woman flicking ash from her Gitane as her terrier peed on a lamppost. I adored the iron street lamps, another relic of a bygone time.

"Ah," said Anton. "To our left, Île Saint-Louis."

I remembered that the Île Saint-Louis was the smaller of the two river islands and more residential than Île de la Cité, our destination.

The Seine was a silt-gray shade that matched the mansard roofs. Even the water was color coordinated with the rest of the city.

"This is the bridge," said Anton. "Pont Marie."

We turned left onto it, passing a vibrant flower market.

"There." Luc pointed just past all the bouquets. "Remember. You take the metro there, to our party."

"Sure thing," Kat said.

I'd already memorized the map, so I wasn't worried about getting lost. A guy on a motorcycle cut us off and Luc spewed profanities, some of which I didn't recognize. For whatever reason, I hadn't imagined so much traffic in Paris. Pedestrians, yes, but not zipping little cars and scooters and the smell of exhaust.

"On Sunday," Anton said, pointing to the colorful blooms, "the flowers turn into birds."

"What kind of birds?" I asked.

He winked at me and said, "Any that you ever want."

As if I only wanted a chirping, pretty thing with wings. A bright canary. No. I wanted my life back. Even if I could never have Vince back, I wanted what Kat had taken from me.

The scene was still vivid in my mind. On the morning of the ACTs, I'd gotten up early and made myself Vince's favorite breakfast: pancakes and bacon, making sure to dip the strips of bacon in maple syrup. And I put plenty of butter on the pancakes, so much that it congealed into yellow globs in the lake of syrup.

Our mom slept in on the weekends she didn't have to work—I suspected that she took an extra dose of sleeping pills—and I had her blessing to take the Escort. Before driving the thirty minutes to Washington High, the closest test site, I checked that I had a handful of sharpened no. 2 pencils and that my calculator was in working order.

I arrived an hour and fifteen minutes early, just in case I had car trouble. I entered through the familiar doors by the gym and walked past the trophy case, the smell of chlorine lingering in the air.

It was late September, and I'd only been in French Club for a few weeks—I'd realized that I needed one more extracurricular for my scholarship applications. I bided my time before the test in the student center/cafeteria, going over my meticulous notes, but knowing that any last-minute studying was basically useless.

I watched as the proctors set up the registration area, and after a few other students began to file in, I walked confidently toward the table labeled "A–D." I didn't think much of the fact that my French classmate and fellow club member Katherine (and pronounced kuh-TREEN) was directly behind me. We said hi, acknowledging each other, but that was the extent of our initial interaction.

I was feeling very confident about the test. I knew that I'd ace the English and reading sections of the exam, so I'd spent most of my time studying for the mathematics and science reasoning portions. I finished the reading and math sections with gusto, given my abilities and preparations. When I was done with that first half, I was sure to go over the Scantron sheet and darken every little oval space that I'd marked.

Halfway through, the proctor let us have a bathroom break. As I was washing my hands at the trough sink, Kat was doing the same.

She looked at me in the mirror and spoke: "You're brilliant. I mean, you finished the section before anyone else. All cool and collected."

"Thanks," I said, flattered by the compliment.

I returned to the testing room, thrilled that Kat had acknowledged my presence. Maybe she wanted to be my friend outside of French Club. After all, she'd said I was cool.

I blazed through the remaining half of the exam.

Weeks later, I received an envelope in the mail. My scores validated my confidence: a perfect 36. I was giddy, euphoric, and hopeful for the future. I'd already prepared the scholarship essays and materials for U of I, UIC, Northern Illinois, and Illinois State, and I sent them off at 5:00 p.m., just in time for the last mail of the afternoon.

The very next day, my guidance counselor (who also happened to be the head football coach) called me into his office. As he told me the problem—that another student at the testing site had also gotten a perfect score and investigators suspected cheating—I stared at the inspirational poster showing a field of alpine wildflowers.

How could this be? And who had had the audacity to copy my answers? This was my ticket to college, my way out of this one-stoplight town. My mom made just above minimum wage. I could work a hundred summers in the Pine Haven cafeteria and still not have enough money for tuition. This was ludicrous—some opportunist was taking advantage of me.

Coach Gilbert told me that the proctor had failed to record the seating arrangement, so the cheater couldn't be identified with certainty. He said that my scores would be cancelled, but I could take the test again. I was too shocked to protest. Someone had cheated off me, but I was also being punished? Even if I'd thought to hire an attorney, I couldn't pay for one.

"We all miss your brother," said Coach Gilbert, blurting a total non sequitur. Without a word, I went back to my physics class.

I fell into despair when I realized that if I took the test again, my scores wouldn't come in time for the scholarship application deadlines in early December. With my confidence shaken, I didn't think it possible to ace the test for a second time.

Several days later, in French class at Wash High, I overheard Kiran teasing Kat about being "perfect." I didn't know what she was referring to until other students started talking about early college acceptance. Kiran would be going to the University of Chicago, the most elite school in the Midwest—private and exorbitantly expensive. But I heard the envy in her voice when she was asking Kat about New Haven.

"I guess it's a slum outside the campus area," Kat said. "Daddy dearest would have a stroke if I didn't follow in his footsteps. And then on to Yale Law."

It wasn't difficult to put the pieces together. Kat was always looking over my shoulder (or Kiran's) during French tests and did poorly on the oral exams—the only test she *couldn't* cheat on. I knew she got good grades in her other courses, and I suspected that she was smart enough to cheat without getting caught.

Why hadn't Coach Gilbert fought for me? Did he see me only as Vince's sister? Prairie didn't have quite the stature of Wash, but I had a perfect academic record, and Kat merely had a good one.

Her father was a big-shot attorney. My absentee dad was working class, a freight conductor. And that made all the difference. But now I held the power. I would ruin her life just as she'd ruined mine.

Luc and Anton dropped us off at our pied-à-terre. We'd written down their address, along with metro directions, and promised to be at their party the following night.

Once they had driven off, Whitney squealed: "Can you believe our luck?"

My companions rolled their bags up to our address, 4 Rue du Cloître-Notre-Dame. We were literally across the street from the flying buttresses of the cathedral. Our side of the block had two gift shops and a café, which looked to be filled with homely tourists rather than chic Parisians. The buildings themselves were stately and uniform, gray stone looming above Notre-Dame. We'd rented a garret apartment on the top floor.

"Wait. Nessa, that's your only luggage?" said Whitney.

Sherlock had finally made a deduction. Kiran had noticed earlier, but I don't think she wanted to pry. She knew my family wasn't as well-off.

"I travel light," I said, by way of explanation.

"Whatever. We need to get some killer outfits for tomorrow night," said Whitney. "My aunt was telling me about this cool store called Tati."

"First things first, princess," Kat said. "Who gets Luc and who gets Anton?"

"If I'm a princess, then you're queen bitch," Whitney shot back.

The apartment entrance was an intricate wrought-iron gate, and right next door was a cheesy souvenir shop called Forever Paris, the whimsical font a direct rip-off from Walt Disney.

"Anton seemed to like *you*," Kiran said to me, her eyes wide in playful accusation.

Whitney read from a Post-it. She punched the door code into the keypad and said it aloud so we could memorize it: "In oh fifteen hundred ninety-two, Columbus didn't sail the ocean blue. You guys got it? 0-1-5-9-2."

"Brilliant," I said, but I wasn't sure if she picked up on the sarcasm.

We were greeted by the sound of a yapping dog. Though the door was covered by a pale lace curtain, I could see a human shadow. A woman with an inch-wide streak of white strands, bright against her dark hair, allowed us in. A fluffy dog the color of vanilla ice cream sniffed our ankles.

"Bonjour, Madame," said Whitney. She was technically the president of French Club, but only because no one else had bothered to run.

The woman responded in kind and then performed the traditional European greeting in three swift motions. I didn't know if we were supposed to simply touch cheeks and kiss the air, or if actual lip-to-cheek contact was expected. It happened too fast. I hated looking stupid.

The lady spoke rapidly and held the keys. We all trudged up four flights of stairs. I really should've offered to help Whitney with all her luggage this time, but that would've been the old me, polite and Goody Two-shoes.

Finally, we reached the top floor and the landlady led us into a cramped, spartan apartment. A short hallway with an all-white bathroom on the right-hand side led to the kitchen. The only bed was tucked under the kitchen alcove. A spider plant on the counter was the single nod to decoration.

The landlady showed us the appliances—a stovetop, toaster oven, and mini fridge—speaking so fast that I didn't understand. The final appliance appeared to be a very compact washing machine. I'd never seen one in a kitchen before. She also presented a fresh baguette in brown paper wrapping, then opened the refrigerator to show a large box of orange juice, a slab of butter, and a jar of berry jam. The dog wagged his poufy tail, looking up at us as if expecting some of the bread.

The living room sported long floor cushions covered in orange-and-red-striped fabric, plus crimson back pillows and a round coffee table, all looking more suited to a cruise ship than an elegant pied-à-terre. I couldn't have designed it better myself. I knew the girls were probably expecting floral toile wallpaper and herringbone floors.

As the landlady handed over the two skeleton keys, I noticed one of the key chains was a pewter Playboy bunny—how crass and un-Parisian and utterly perfect. The other was one of those mini Swiss Army knives. She left us to unpack.

"How delightfully tacky," said Kat. "How much are we paying for this?"

"Come on, it's kind of cute," Kiran said.

"So I noticed that Anton was into *you*," Kat echoed. "Why in fuck's sake did you blow him off?"

"Not my type," I replied. "Instead of hurting his precious feelings, I told him I like girls."

"And how do we know that's not true?"

This was more difficult to explain. "I just have specific taste in men."

Kat seemed satisfied by my answer. "Fair enough."

"I think the virgin should get the hottest guy," I said, thinking this might provoke an argument.

We all looked at Kiran.

"You're right," said Kat.

Sometimes my aim was off. I was a virgin, too, but I'd lied before and said I'd slept with a guy named Adam at summer camp. As if my family could afford summer camp.

"Yeah, Kir-bear," Whitney said. "Let's get you devirginized. The rest of us can fight over Luc."

I was pleased by the possibility of a battle between Kat and Whitney. But I couldn't resist adding: "Ted Bundy was handsome and charming. I mean, what if they're serial killers?"

I got a sarcastic "thanks, Eeyore" in return. I told them they were very welcome. Anytime.

We then played rock-paper-scissors to see who would share the bed and who'd get the striped cushions. I won the first round and rights to the bed. Unfortunately, Kat won the second round, so I'd have to share a mattress with that Uma Thurman wannabe.

The other girls lobbied for naps before venturing out. We'd planned to go to the Louvre on our first day, but since that wasn't an option, they wanted to go to Notre-Dame and walk around the Latin Quarter to find the café where students from the Sorbonne gathered. I wanted to see Père Lachaise, but I was outnumbered.

I didn't intend to sleep, but I also didn't want to leave and have them explore the city without me. So I explored the confines of our pied-à-terre. The hall closet contained lots of hangers, a pair of sheets, and a canister vacuum. The kitchen cupboards, mostly bare, held a bottle of brandy, what appeared to be a jar of sundried tomatoes, three packets of asparagus soup, a book of matches, and a half-empty bottle of sunflower seed oil, judging by the label.

It finally dawned on me to look through their bags for possible intel to exploit. The problem was that the sound of the zipper might wake them. The front pocket of Kat's rolling suitcase gaped open to reveal several lacy black thongs. No surprise there. But I did find a thin stack of white notecards, held together with a ponytail band. As I started to read them, I couldn't believe my luck. They were a series of hokey affirmations: *I am beautiful inside and out. I am unique and worthy of love. I am intelligent and capable of great things. I am never alone.*

This was a gold mine. I slipped them into my messenger bag for future use. Because I wanted to try a cigarette at some point—when I was alone and wouldn't make a fool of myself by coughing or doing it incorrectly—I filched a pack of her Marlboro Lights.

The front pocket of her suitcase also contained a half bottle of Prozac, prescribed to one Katherine Anne Cahill. What could she possibly be depressed about? She had everything, right down to her salon-perfect hair.

I'd known about the antidepressants. When French Club had met at Kat's McMansion, I'd gone into her bathroom and rummaged through the medicine cabinet, hoping to find valuable information, maybe even vulnerability. What kind of teenage girl has her own bathroom? A rich one, that's who.

I was tempted to throw away her pills or even switch them out for some the same shape and color, something innocuous like acid reflux meds. I had easy access to other medications at Pine Haven, especially when my mom worked the night shift. But I couldn't do it.

I felt a pang of regret for missing my chance—the good girl in me was that nagging angel on my shoulder. But denying Kat her happy pills wasn't the best revenge anyway, I reasoned. She had to know what she'd done to me and that she'd ruined my entire future. And I would be the ghost that haunted hers.

I watched her sleeping, a pearl of spit forming at the side of her mouth. To sleep was to be exposed and vulnerable—I knew this too well. The first and only slumber party I'd attended had been back in seventh grade, and I'd only been invited because I was Vince's sister. Little did I know, I was also the evening's entertainment.

We'd played Truth or Dare. I remember being paralyzed with fear—should I choose truth, in which case I'd probably have to reveal that I had a crush on Justin Stotz, the most popular boy in our grade, or dare, and endure some unknown act of humiliation? At the time, it didn't occur to me that I could lie.

Dare seemed safer. They dared me to call Andy Wetherington, the second most popular boy in our grade (and the birthday girl's boyfriend) and say that I was in love with him. I dialed and as I tried to formulate words, my voice cracked. So I hung up.

The next morning I woke up to find the word "LESBO" written across my forehead in blue Magic Marker and little red hearts drawn on my arms. I cried for days.

As a silver lining to that dark cloud, I'd learned quite a bit about this so-called game. Not only was it a confessional in disguise, but each dare was tailored to pinpoint the individual girl's weaknesses. I realized that it was perfect for our Parisian adventures.

I told myself that my travel companions would be easy to crack—one and done. I'd learned from French Club that Kat was competitive and reckless, a dangerous combination. Whitney wanted to be our leader, and to be the most popular, so desperately that she'd do almost anything to prove it. And Kiran just liked to see everyone happy, because her own happiness hinged upon that of the group. If we were having fun with the game, she would, too.

At the right time, we could play Truth, and I'd make Kat confess her cheating. I'd also humiliate her with the "truth" of her cheesy affirmations.

And think of the dares! This way, I could get Kat alone somewhere on the Eiffel Tower and dare her to climb one of the girders with me. I'd disclose my secret and meet my end, right in front of her eyes.

Let the game begin.

As we walked past Notre-Dame, even I could recognize its Gothic glory. I liked the stone gargoyles, those monstrous beasts. The cathedral might've been more magnificent without the hordes of sunburned tourists, including lots of Americans in khakis and fanny packs, all trying to get the best-possible photo. We decided to hit the cathedral on our way back, hoping it'd be less crowded by evening.

Crossing the Petit Pont, we walked along the tree-lined Quai de Montebello. The block had a bike shop, cafés, and the famed bookstore Shakespeare and Company, which featured English-language books. I made a mental note to come back alone to browse since the other girls wouldn't be interested.

Haussmann hadn't wreaked quite as much havoc in the Latin Quarter, for we found a few narrow streets no bigger than one-lane alleys. Some of the buildings bore his stamp, and nearly all were constructed of the cream-colored limestone and featured French windows.

It was difficult not to be distracted by the Parisian women. Their high-heeled shoes clicked on the sidewalks, a sharp, staccato announcement: *I am a beautiful woman!* Like the elegant mademoiselle who wore a navy suit with matching patent-leather pumps, an abstract-print scarf knotted at the base of her swan neck, her mahogany hair in a chignon, and a kiss of matte red lipstick. I longed to be her, to be comfortable in my own skin, to move through the world with ease. But I didn't have to try any longer, because I would be leaving this world for another.

Suddenly I was famished and annoyed that I had to take care of such corporeal needs. We'd agreed upon Café Saint-Jacques, where, according to the guidebook, students from the Sorbonne liked to hang out.

"Let's get wine," Whitney said. "And get drunk with college guys!"

It was a rare occasion that I agreed with her. But we'd somehow lost Kat and Kiran.

"Hey, wait," said Kiran, nearly ten feet behind us.

"Gross," said Kat, staring at one of Kiran's New Balance crosstrainers, which was now covered in dog shit.

"That was from a wolfhound or a Doberman," I said, just to rub it in. "A big dog."

"You know, Nessa," said Kat, "you were practically mute in class. Turns out you're pretty funny."

I am funny, I thought, *but you didn't know that because you haven't bothered to get to know me.*

"Here," Whitney said. "Just, like, lean on me so you can scrape it off, okay?"

"My only other shoes are flip-flops," Kiran said, her voice sounding far away. "My only pair. My favorites. That's why I wore them."

Kat, to my dismay, showed some humanity: "Come on. We need to get you some fuck-me heels anyway. Stilettos and that hottie Anton. Kiss that virginity good-bye."

While I was pleased to see Kiran's dose of reality, I was more disturbed than I'd expected by her response. It was like seeing the Easter Bunny cry.

Café Saint-Jacques turned out to be closed. Given the fickle nature of the French, I should've expected as much. We settled for Chez Marguerite, a café closer to the river. Kiran said she wanted a drink as soon as possible.

"Should we get a bottle of something?" Whitney asked as we were being seated. All of the outdoor tables were occupied, so we had to settle for inside. The interior felt quintessentially French, with warm wood panels, antique mirrors, and white tablecloths.

When a young waiter approached, Whitney asked for a bottle of the house rosé, pronouncing it "rose," like the flower.

"Le rosé?" he said, emphasizing the second syllable. *"Je crois que vous parlez de* rosé.*"*

Tears welled in Whitney's eyes. I hoped we weren't in for a spectacle. I just wanted to have a decent meal, free of drama.

"We'll take two bottles, then," Kat said, reverting to English. "Dickweed."

Upon hearing the insult, he smirked—I assumed that he spoke decent English. I was almost charmed by Kat's loyalty to Whitney. If only she'd thought twice before screwing me over. Whitney, for her part, appeared to be fortified by Kat's words.

The asshole waiter returned with two bottles and an ice bucket. He poured a glass for each of us, corked the nearly empty bottle, set it on the table, and left the full bottle in the ice.

"Cheers?" I said.

"Cheers," Kiran said. *"Salut."*

"I'd toast to Paris," Whitney added, "but I don't think it deserves a toast yet."

"Hence my tentative suggestion," I said, wanting to say that Paris was temperamental and capricious, just like life. The wine tasted crisp and refreshing. I liked it more than I'd expected.

The arrogant waiter took our orders. Whitney asked for a *salade niçoise*, no anchovies. I wanted a *croque madame* while Kat ordered the beef bourguignon with *pommes frites*. When Kiran said she wanted a *croque monsieur*, I warned her that it contained ham, because she was a strict vegetarian. I wondered if she was a little drunk already.

"I know it has ham," Kiran said. "That's the point. What happens in Paris stays in Paris."

"That's the spirit!" Kat cried.

I was encouraged by Kiran's statement. She seemed more willing to take risks and abandon her values, at least while here. I hoped she'd be disabused of that relentless optimism soon.

The conversation gravitated toward what we'd do tomorrow. I wanted to see Père Lachaise, and Kat lobbied for the sex museum—leave it to Kat to find a museum devoted to eroticism. Kiran and Whitney reminded us about Tati, the discount department store where we could find outfits and shoes, which also happened to be very close to Montmartre and the sex museum. I told them we should take the metro to Barbès–Rochechouart, based on the guidebook's map, and we could hit the Musée de l'Érotisme, Montmartre, and Tati all in one fell swoop. Then, in the afternoon, the famed cemetery. And finally, the party. The Eiffel Tower would have to wait until the following day.

As I poured more wine for everyone, the hand holding the bottle seemed disconnected from my body. I was definitely tipsy. Empty stomach, I figured.

"I want to try rabbit while I'm here," said Kiran.

I began to sing that kids' song, complete with hand motions: *"Little Bunny Foo Foo, hoppin' through the forest, scoopin' up the field mice and boppin' 'em on the head."*

"You are out of control," Kiran said, laughing. Hearing Kiran laugh made me happy and warm. I couldn't really feel my own lips. Was I going soft?

"There, my friend, you are wrong." I pointed my index finger at Kiran. "I am in complete control. I am not long for this world."

"I'm not long for the French," said Kat. "But I hope I can find a long Frenchman."

I giggled because this was one of the funniest things I'd ever heard. But I had to get myself together. Eyes on the prize. While I loved the fuzziness of my first drunken experience, I needed to be sharper to be most effective.

Kat and Whitney didn't even seem tipsy. They'd probably been drunk enough times that they could hold their alcohol. I didn't want them to wield any power over me, so I had to take it easy on the wine.

The waiter brought our meals without fanfare. Whitney stared at her salad, which had five anchovies nestled on top.

"Eww," she said, disgusted by the little fish on her plate.

How could I exploit this situation? Meanwhile, Kat ate her beef bourguignon with gusto and Kiran picked at her open-faced ham and cheese sandwich, mostly eating the cheese.

"You should hide an anchovy somewhere," Kat said, in between bites. "It'll rot and smell horrible. My cousin put a shrimp in the curtains once. Drove my mom and the cleaning lady crazy trying to find the source."

Of course Kat had a cleaning lady.

"I have gum," I said, accidentally slurring the last word. "You can use it, stick one under the table. Here, everybody chew a piece."

Emboldened, the girls accepted the Winterfresh gum and chewed diligently.

I said, "We should just, like, skip out on the bill. These assholes don't deserve our money."

Kiran frowned. "We can't do that. Can we?"

I remembered: Truth or Dare. I focused on the gum, asking for everyone's contribution and wadding it into a ball. I stuck it to an anchovy and put it under the table, making sure the gum held fast.

Then I said the magic words: "Dare you. I dare all of you to run out on the bill."

"Let's do it. On three?"

I don't remember who said it; nor do I particularly care. It was a turning point. It was the first sinister act of the trip. We all rose from the table, leaving our napkins on our chairs, and strode to the door.

"Dickweed," I said, smiling. A wave of euphoria crashed over my body, an intense giddiness. Ahead of us, I could see the sun sparkling over the river. But I knew better than to trust this feeling.

As the cliché goes, there's not a day that goes by when I don't think of her. When she appears in my dreams, I find joy, because she's alive and well. But then I wake, and the weight of reality crushes my chest, suffocating me until the Klonopin kicks in. If a doctor prescribes it, it's not really addiction—at least that's how I rationalize things.

I feel doubly guilty that I rarely see Vince in my slumber. But she is always there, often lurking in the periphery, always floating around the edges of my subconscious.

I wasn't a complete monster—I was just a teenage girl. At least that's what I tell myself.

We exited Chez Marguerite in triumph, having left without footing the bill. I felt light and effervescent. In all likelihood, my euphoria was a direct result of the alcohol coursing through my veins like bubbly magic.

Fortunately, lots of tourists were out that evening, and we blended into the crowd. On the bridge, a street performer crooned an a cappella version of that Elvis song "Can't Help Falling in Love." Hearing Elvis in Paris felt wrong, like starting up the stairs with my left foot.

"Wise men say only fools rush in . . ."

That was exactly right. Only idiots believed in love. The busker could've at least chosen Serge Gainsbourg, but he must've been getting more tips with Elvis. *Stupid Americans,* I thought, and laughed aloud. I still had a buzz from the wine.

"I can't believe we just did that," said Kiran.

"Seriously? That's nothing. Just foreplay," Kat said. She'd lit up a cigarette and was blowing the smoke through her nose.

"We can do much, much better," I said, staring out over the Seine. A white tour boat cruised through the water. The sun had fallen lower in the sky, a bright egg yolk, casting a glow on the regal buildings lining the river. The gray stone took on a pinkish hue. Even I had to admit how romantic it seemed—Paris was showing her alluring side, warming from the starker shades of black and white. I suspected the rosé was literally coloring my perspective.

"Speaking of foreplay, I need to get my fuck on," said Kat. "And I need to figure out which guys are straight and which ones are gay."

"You're such a nymph," said Whitney, flipping her large Jackie O sunglasses atop her head. They served to hold back her long blonde locks.

"I think you mean nympho. Unless you're referring to the nature spirit in Greek mythology." I was sure that my knowledge was annoying to the people I corrected, but I just couldn't let the error stand. Besides, I didn't mind annoying Whitney as long as I didn't make her cry.

Kat had a point about the guys here. I focused my attention on the passing men who weren't tourists. One guy sucked on a cigarette, wearing a dark, low-necked T-shirt and slouchy stocking cap, like a modern beat poet. Another guy walked in the opposite direction, wearing a salmon-pink linen suit, cut high at the ankles, with white loafers. I was confused. In the States, he'd be gay, no question. But here, all the guys seemed stylish. Most were buffed, manicured, and polished. The next one that caught my eye had aquiline features, an Hermès briefcase, and a silk scarf knotted around his neck.

But what did I care about helping Kat? I was here to destroy her.

Kiran spoke, an almost confidential whisper, her question directed toward my nemesis: "Don't you have a boyfriend?"

Kat snorted. "I don't even know what to call Christopher. 'Lover' sounds too formal and 'fuckbuddy' is too juvenile. 'Sex friend'?"

From what Kat had mentioned before, Christopher worked in her father's law firm, was married with infant twin boys, and was recently made partner. She'd shown us a photo—he wasn't gorgeous or anything. I didn't understand the appeal.

"We get it," Whitney said. "You're not, like, exclusive."

I was still listening to the Elvis impersonator. He was pretty good, to be honest. He'd moved on to "Hound Dog," which described Whitney to a T.

"Ooh, we should go on a river cruise," suggested Kiran. She had one hand on the stone ledge of the bridge for balance, and the other held her foot as she stretched her quads. I wasn't sure if I should remind her about the dog shit.

"But I get really seasick," said Whitney. "And with this wine, um, yeah."

"Too bad. The guidebook calls it 'absolutely stunning.'" I'd never actually been on a boat before. The opportunity had never presented itself.

"Then let's go inside Notre-Dame," said Kiran. The rosé made her more enthusiastic than usual. "There's hardly a line now."

We agreed, and walked through the square. Other visitors craned their necks and lifted their cameras to get the perfect shot of the great cathedral. Being older than most of the other structures in the city, the church was a rather unappealing smoky beige, as if tarnished by centuries of pollution. The medieval Gothic architecture was sharp and biting, all angles and points, much like I imagined torture chambers of the time. I wanted to see the interior, if only to examine why this place had captured the world's imagination.

"Oh!" Kiran said. "It's Point Zéro! We should get pictures with Notre-Dame in the background." She was referring to the inlaid gold star that marked the point from which all distances were measured in France. In kilometers, of course. The Île de la Cité was the site of the primitive village of the Parisii people when Julius Caesar arrived. For all intents and purposes, it had been the center of Paris ever since.

Kiran handed me her camera, a fancy Olympus, and asked for a photo.

I obliged, saying, *"Dites fromage! Un, deux, trois."*

Kiran beamed, a genuine, happy smile made even wider from the wine.

"I get it!" Whitney shouted. "You said 'say cheese'!"

Kat started clapping, slowly at first, then with increasing speed. "Bravo, Whit, bravo."

Brava, I thought. Italian, the feminine of bravo.

"Oh, bite me, bitch," said Whitney, who then insisted on a photo. She had a disposable camera, one with a little plastic wheel that you had to click forward to advance the film.

In the end, even Kat wanted a picture (taken with her professional-grade Nikon). I hadn't bothered to bring a camera—I wouldn't have wasted film on Notre-Dame anyway. I was thankful my parents hadn't inflicted church on me. Back in middle-school English class, when we'd studied the gods and goddesses of Greek mythology, I hadn't understood why the religious kids weren't questioning everything. Wasn't Christianity also mythology, with their virgin who miraculously gave birth to a god?

I also remembered how, in second grade, I overheard some of the girls talking about first Communion at recess. While they were swinging on the monkey bars, they spoke of drinking grape juice that was Jesus's blood. I was both horrified and terrified—the only creatures who drank blood were vampires. Confusion ensued. As I stood in front of Our Lady of Paris, I still didn't fully understand how transubstantiation worked. No wonder that, during the Revolution, Notre-Dame was renamed the "Temple of Reason."

"Are those the bell towers?" Whitney asked, pointing toward the western façade. "There's Quasimodo!"

"What?" Kat said.

"Ha," Whitney gloated. "Made you look."

I hadn't seen the Disney movie that had come out a few years back, but I'd read the Victor Hugo novel. I suspected that any animated version was both oversimplified and sanitized.

"I kind of wanted Quasimodo and Esmeralda to end up together," said Kiran wistfully. "Phoebus was too perfect."

"They *did* end up together," I said. "In death, but still."

Whitney whirled around. "What are you talking about?"

"The novel," I said. "After Esmeralda is executed—"

"In the book they burn her?" interrupted Whitney.

"No, they hang her," I said. "And then Quasimodo goes to the graveyard of unclaimed bodies and refuses to leave her corpse. He starves to death."

"That's weirdly romantic," said Kiran. "But it doesn't surprise me that Disney changed the ending. That's not exactly kid tested, mother approved."

"Choosy moms choose life!" Kat shouted. "Cheer up, Whit. We all die."

How true, I thought. But most of us aren't responsible for another's demise. Only the wicked, like Kat.

As we got closer to the cathedral, I could see the gallery of kings lining the space above the three portals. During the Revolution, they'd been decapitated, then later restored. Some of the gargoyles were less conspicuous. Once I spotted them, I was impressed by the winged, serpentine creatures that jutted outward, their mouths gaping open to divert the rainwater. Some had fangs or piercing beaks. They were strange and wonderful.

I could have spent hours staring at the architecture, but I had to keep the momentum of the game going. The next dare needed to be a little more subversive than the last. But it couldn't be designated for Kat, not yet. I had to make her think that the first few were just a warm-up so that Kat's challenges were more audacious and bold. If she could appeal to my vanity—I could still hear her voice from the day of the ACT, slithering compliments, "You're brilliant . . . all cool and collected"—then I could appeal to hers.

The four of us didn't have to wait long before we were allowed to file inside the cathedral. I knew I'd be amused to see what sinners had built to appease God.

Inside, my eyes had to adjust to the relative darkness.

The stained-glass windows let in almost no light. Around us, people craned their necks and spoke in hushed tones. The vaulted ceiling, supported by grand pillars, soared at least three stories over our heads. Though ornate chandeliers illuminated some of the space, much of the cathedral fell in shadow. It felt cold and ominous.

A security guard moved us through the entry gate, where we'd stopped to gaze. He pointed to the placard showing the symbol of a camera flash, covered by a giant X. If the other girls took any photos, the exposures would be too dark.

"Hey, if we get separated, meet here?" Kiran said, pointing to the universal white stick figure on a green background. "*Sortie* means exit. Remember that."

"Sure thing, Mom," said Kat.

"Shhh." Whitney tapped on the sign that announced "Silence" in many different languages, most prominently in English.

Rows of square wooden chairs—I'd expected pews—led up to the main altar, which featured a giant white cross with several bouquets of pale flowers. Worst of all, I couldn't get away from the grotesque crucifixes. All of the tortured, writhing green corpses of Jesus looked the same to me. How did an awful, torturous death become the symbol of a religion? I was all for reality, but this seemed a bit much—and this was all an elaborate myth, anyway.

A smell I didn't recognize—frankincense or myrrh, maybe— lingered in the air. In the side chapels, candles flickered in fiery clusters. I wondered how long it would take for the cathedral to go up in flames—it was mostly stone, so it would be a slow burn. What would be saved first? The altar? One of the many crucifixes?

"This is killing my buzz," Kat said as we wandered around the side chapels.

I hated to admit it, but I agreed with Kat. Another emaciated cadaver hovered above us. My neck hurt from looking upward so much. In front of us, Kiran and Whitney stopped in front of the huge circle of stained glass, one of the rose windows. At first glance, the multicolored glass, a giant kaleidoscope of wonder, was magnificent. But as I looked closer, I could see each part of the window was composed of tiny biblical scenes. Both Whitney and Kiran took photos, dutifully, without the flash.

"A lot of religions are strange," Kiran said. She seemed genuinely contemplative. She'd never talked about being religious, but I assumed that she was Hindu.

In any case, it was more buzzkill for me. How could I make this stop? I wondered whether to focus on Kiran or Whitney for the next dare.

Kat responded to Kiran's statement about religion with a quote from *Pulp Fiction*: "Ezekiel 25:17. The path of the righteous man is beset on all sides by the inequities of the selfish and the tyranny of evil men—"

"Men?" I snapped. I was so sick of her bullshit—everything about her was plagiarized, from her canned responses to her signature look. "Do you have to be gender specific? Tell me about the awesome women in that movie. That's actually a rhetorical question, because there aren't any. Besides, religion is the opiate of the people."

"I forgot," Kat said. "You know everything."

Damn right, I thought. "Not everything. Just more than you."

"God works in mysterious ways," Whitney said, shrugging. "I think there's something bigger than us."

Here I found myself agreeing with Whitney. I did believe there was something greater than ourselves, but I didn't think it could be found in organized religion. I knew that when I died I would see Vince, because I was a good person, and even if good people weren't rewarded on earth, we'd be rewarded on another plane.

"I think you're right," said Kiran to Whitney, without further elaboration. I couldn't remember if Hindus believed in reincarnation.

We stopped at the stone effigy of Joan of Arc. I shuddered as I recalled Joan's demise—burned at the stake, of course. From the inscribed dates, I calculated the martyr's age: nineteen. Just a year older than we were. I couldn't imagine the excruciating pain, the flames searing her skin, every nerve screaming, her outer layers blackened like meat on a barbecue.

"What a horrible way to go," Kat said. "I'd much rather be beheaded. Quicker and less painful."

"Mmm." I traced my lips with my index finger. "I'd walk the plank. Or jump from a high place, because you have a massive heart attack midair."

Whitney said, "She's not very feminine looking, is she?"

"I don't think it matters," I replied, "if you're a badass."

I studied Joan's stoic face. Strong jaw. Armor and a tunic-style dress, which in her time could've just as easily been a man's tunic. And Joan held her sword at her side. In order to fight, she had to look like any other soldier. Like a man. And despite her victory, she was executed by fire, which I imagined to be the worst death possible.

I willed myself to focus on the task at hand—a dare for Whitney or Kiran. *Better to begin small and build up to the climax,* I thought. *Start with a match and some newspaper kindling to ignite the giant conflagration.*

I set my sights on Whitney, who believed in God. I'd noticed that she had, ever so slightly, made the sign of the cross when we'd entered. She was Catholic, no doubt. I vaguely remembered last spring when she'd come to French class with ash on her forehead.

We were passing another side chapel full of candles when the brilliant idea struck me.

"Hey, Whit," I said, pointing toward the flames. "I dare you to light a cigarette on one of those."

Kat gave me a high five. *Oh, what that bitch doesn't know,* I thought. And then she whipped out a Marlboro Light from her purse. I doubt she'd even notice a pack was missing from her luggage.

"But those are prayers," Whitney protested, "and some of them are for dead people."

"Just put it in your mouth," Kat said, keeping a straight face. "Now light it."

All Whitney had to do was belly up to the candles and inhale.

"What if these people died," she said, the cigarette hanging from the side of her mouth, "in horrible ways?"

So maybe the girl was more empathetic than I gave her credit for. That meant that I'd have to put more thought into her reeducation. In acclimating her to the small sufferings in life.

"Oh my God," Whitney said. "We're all going to hell."

"See you there, sister," said Kat.

How accurate! She was destined for an unpleasant fate. Not that I really believed in hell. But I did believe that bad people ended up in limbo, a *Groundhog Day* type of scenario where they had to relive the same day, over and over.

When Whitney pulled away from the bouquet of candles, it was clear the cigarette wasn't lit.

"You have to inhale a little bit, dumbass," said Kat. "Try again."

This should be good, I thought. As Whitney leaned in to greet the flame, several strands of her long blonde locks fell in front of her face and dripped into the fire. The gag-inducing smell of burning hair surrounded us.

Whitney reeled backward, swallowing her scream, which sounded like hiccups. Kiran used two hands to rub out the smoldering bit of hair.

Jesus, I thought, *they're hopeless.* But I was enjoying the spectacle. By that point, several tourists were pointing at us, and Kat linked arms with Whitney and Kiran. I was right behind them, deliriously happy at this turn of events.

"Rule number one," Kat said as we exited the cathedral, "do *not* get arrested."

"I lost, like, two inches of hair!" wailed Whitney, holding the few strands in her fingers. "It's black at the tip!"

"Whit," said Kat. "I swear to God if you don't shut up right now, you're going to get us all in trouble. You lost the amount of a paintbrush. Chill the fuck out."

The twilight accosted us, brighter than I'd expected, as we emerged from the Gothic darkness of Notre-Dame.

I ended up watching *Pulp Fiction* more times than I could count when I was pregnant with Cricket. While the stylized violence repulsed me, I couldn't take my eyes away. Most of all, I was fascinated by the story line of Jules's redemption. Could I, too, be forgiven, despite my sins?

At one point I looked up Ezekiel 25:17 in a King James Bible. To my surprise, I learned Jules hadn't recited the actual verse. His version (which is to say, Tarantino's version) was more nuanced and eloquent: "The path of the righteous man is beset on all sides by the inequities of the selfish . . ."

The first time I saw the movie, before Paris, I identified with Jules—I was the righteous. After Paris, I was acutely aware that I was among the selfish. To this day, I have a difficult time admitting exactly what I did. But Cricket's affinity for all things French and gentle insistence on visiting Paris—she's been saving her allowance since she was five—has reopened an old wound. If I don't take action, I fear I'll lose too much blood.

I looked back to check if anyone was following us out of the cathedral, which, fortunately, wasn't the case. A nun or some woman affiliated with Notre-Dame had yelled at us in French never to come back as we were leaving, but that was the extent of our punishment. They probably had more important things to do.

"I can't believe we got away with it," Kiran said, as if reading my mind. *"Again."*

"Let's get crêpes," Kat suggested. She was always hungry, and like other women of means, she seemed to have the metabolism of a gazelle, but also large breasts. Such a lucky bitch, on so many levels.

"We have to try this place on the Right Bank that I read about," said Kiran.

"Yeah, but there's a crêperie right there." Kat pointed to the café on the corner.

"What about my hair?" Whitney's refrain was grating.

"Tuck it behind your ear," I suggested. "You can't even tell."

It was actually fairly obvious, but I didn't want to deal with Whitney's whining or the very real possibility that she'd burst into tears. So none of us dwelled on the chunk of hair that was missing, nor the more obvious singed ends, coal black against her champagne-blonde hair.

I could go for a crêpe—I had a sweet tooth, and I'd leave this earth soon enough, so why not enjoy the time I had left? The smell of the hot griddle made saliva pool on my tongue. I noted the big jar of Nutella, which I'd never had but wanted to try. I knew it was made from chocolate and hazelnuts, and it was only available at specialty grocers in the States.

The bitchy counter girl didn't dampen Kat's enthusiasm for dessert. She ordered four crêpes with the works: Nutella, bananas, coconut, and Grand Marnier. She also told us to trust her—these were the best kind. I was annoyed by her presumption. How could she know what's best for *me*?

Holding the warm pancake in its paper cuff, I couldn't resist taking a bite before we stumbled to the park behind the cathedral. Bliss. The heavenly hazelnut chocolate oozed on my tongue. The bananas added a fruity sweetness, while the coconut gave a slight crunch. The touch of orange Grand Marnier was sublime. It was difficult to believe this was an earthly delight. And that Kat was right.

I squeezed onto a green bench with the rest of the girls, chewing all the while. Pigeons nosed around the gravel at our feet.

"Oh my God," said Whitney. "I think I just had, like, a Nutella orgasm."

"Have you even had a real one?" Kat taunted.

"Yeah, I have. Why?" Whitney was on the defensive.

Fight, I thought. *Go, Whit, go!*

"So what did it feel like? Describe, please," said Kat, her carefully penciled eyebrow arched.

"Like an explosion," Whitney said. "A bomb of joy."

"I stand corrected. But if a chocolate orgasm feels anything like a real orgasm, you're not doing it right."

I assumed sex was overrated, just like most things in this life. I'd almost finished my crêpe—it was so delicious.

"I forgot," Whitney said, "that you're the orgasm police."

"A bomb of joy?" Kiran asked. "I could use one of those."

"What, you've never had one by yourself?" Kat said, still chewing. "How do you even know what you like, then?"

Kiran shrugged.

It seemed a fair question, but I'd never explored my body, either. Mostly it was just an annoyance, my period something to be dealt with every month (or couple of months). I didn't have breasts to speak of. I was somewhat curious to know what the fuss was about, but not curious enough to make sex—with myself or anyone else—a priority. Maybe I would've slept with my crush, Miah, but he'd made sure that wasn't an option.

I watched the street performers in the park, scoffing at the King Tut over to my right. All he had to do was put on a gold sheet, some gold makeup, and a mask, then stand still. Where was the skill and artistry? Tourists took his photo like it was a big deal and left coins in the box at his feet.

To my left, a mime pretended to fall and dusted himself off. He silently flirted with the crowd, offering a nonexistent bouquet of flowers to a woman wearing a fanny pack. He bended on one knee as if proposing. When she pointed to her wedding ring, he acted heartbroken and ready to kill himself. How goddamn cheesy. Throughout the performance, his white makeup remained flawless.

"So would you rather be raped or murdered?" I asked the girls.

"Kill me, no question," said Kat. "Being raped would be the worst thing ever. Worst I could imagine. You?"

"Rape," I replied. "I want control over my own death."

"This conversation *really* took a turn, Ness," Kiran said, and made a show of wiping her own mouth.

I used the back of my hand to swipe my lips.

Kat lost her patience and intervened. "Nessa, darling, your mouth looks like the brown starfish in your undies."

This sent everyone but me into fits of laughter. So I'd enjoyed myself a bit too much. I didn't think that was very funny. I wanted to be noticed, but not for humiliating reasons.

"I bet you've done anal. Am I right, nympho?" said Whitney, emphasizing the last syllable.

Kat smirked. "Sex is like chocolate, and chocolate's always good. But sometimes you have a craving for something that's normally gross, like a chili cheese dog. And it can be very satisfying."

I was glad the conversation (and their attention) had been diverted from me.

Kiran appeared skeptical. "I still want to try the chocolate before the chili cheese dog. Ooh! That reminds me of a good dare. Nessa, I dare you to eat two more crêpes in the next five minutes."

Poor, sweet, naïve Kiran. A child could have concocted her dare. An eating challenge? We'd have to be gentle with her first act of daring.

"Fine," I said. "Easy peasy."

Kat took the initiative to order the crêpes and bring them back to the park while we watched the mime. He started making an elaborate faux picnic for his beloved, throwing out a blanket and opening a basket of food. Then he carefully buttered the bread and began to chew.

"Bon appétit," said Kat, handing over the crêpes.

Kiran had a sports watch, so she appointed herself as time-keeper: "Ready?"

I tore into the first one, not caring about the Nutella all over my face. If they wanted a show, they'd get one. I downed it in a minute thirty.

"Don't worry, Kir-bear," said Kat. "We'll make sure you get some of Anton's chocolate tomorrow night at the party."

I detected a hint of blush blooming under Kiran's dark skin.

The second crêpe proved to be more difficult. By minute four, my stomach was queasy from the combination of rich dessert and lingering rosé. But I was determined to complete the dare.

At four minutes, forty-five seconds, I wiped the last bit of coconut stuck to my cheek. Success.

"Damn, girl," said Kat. "That was impressive."

I'm not here to impress you, I thought.

I was within two feet of the green trash can before the vomit rose in my throat.

I needed more information about their vulnerabilities—I had to expedite the truth portion of the game, and I figured more alcohol would help. Since we'd already agreed upon tomorrow's itinerary, I had to get them to agree to the Eiffel Tower for the next day. That would give me about thirty-six hours until showtime. Whitney wanted to go back to the apartment to fix her hair, and I wanted to brush my teeth to get rid of the puke taste in my mouth. Darkness was falling, and I think we all felt the pull of exhaustion as we hiked up the stairs.

I knew the girls would be less likely to confess in public, so I had to find a way to keep them in the apartment rather than head to a bar. Then I remembered the brandy in the cupboard. It'd have to suffice.

I took a swig of the brandy straight from the bottle. *Drinkable,* I thought. It'd do to keep their buzz going.

"Hey," Kat said. "Share!"

"What's it taste like?" asked Kiran.

I handed the booze to Kat and looked for shot glasses, but no dice. I lined up four juice glasses in a row so the rims touched, as

I'd seen a bartender do on TV. Kat let the spout of the bottle fall, watching the golden liquid slosh into the cups.

Whitney emerged from the bathroom, her eyes red and puffy, snot dripping from her nose. She started to hiccup and sob at the same time.

"No," Kat said. "There's no crying in Paris!"

Finally, I thought, *someone else who gets how much life sucks.* I liked the way the brandy warmed my throat and made my head feel light.

Kat ordered Whitney to drink up. When Whitney hesitated, Kat took the fourth glass and tipped it up to Whitney's lips. She did start to drink, which was a relief. I wanted Whitney to be uncomfortable, but her bawling was painful to hear.

"Here, I have some bobby pins," said Kiran. She took the burned strands and tucked them behind Whitney's ear, securing everything with two bobby pins. "You can't even tell."

You could, actually, because the singed ends stuck out just below her ear, like a feathery black earring.

"So we've done a few dares. Now we need to play Truth," I said, trying to usher everyone into the living area, which could hardly be called a room. I brought the bottle of brandy with me.

The cushions weren't particularly comfortable, and a small lamp provided the only light, but I figured the cover of darkness might make them feel safer. If I could get Whitney talking, she'd be less likely to continue crying.

"So Whitney," I said. "What's the worst thing you've ever done?"

"The worst thing I've ever done, huh?" Whitney took a sip of her brandy before continuing. "This brandy is kind of gross. But okay, fine, I'll be brutally honest. My sister Ashley's gorgeous, right? Always has been. Never went through an awkward stage. She was the smart one, too. And a varsity track star. But a super-deep sleeper.

"So when I was like fourteen, I faked an interest in my neighbor's dog-grooming business. I borrowed her cordless clippers, the really quiet kind for jumpy dogs, because I told her I wanted to practice on our Yorkie. One night, after Ashley's asleep—she sleeps like a corpse—I shaved off her eyebrows. I wanted to shave off her perfect blonde hair, but I didn't."

I found this rather amusing—the pot calling the kettle black. Whitney had long, naturally blonde hair, the color of a golden ale. With the exception of the burned patch.

Whitney stopped for a second, looking upward. "I just wanted her to be ugly for once."

"You devious little bitch," said Kat. "I love it."

Good one, Kat, I thought. *Just you wait.* I remembered the affirmation notecards in my messenger bag, but it was too early to reveal my hand. I wanted to scream, *No, Kat, you are not unique! You are not worthy of love. And you're certainly not beautiful inside and out.*

"Kiran," I said. "Same question."

"I hate my parents," Kiran blurted.

"Ooh, Kiran, you're so naughty," Kat said, working on her second brandy.

"No, I mean it," Kiran said. "I really hate them. My dad's an internist and moonlights in the ER to save money for my med school tuition. Because that's what the world needs, right? Another Indian doctor. They didn't have a son, so I'm expected to take care of them when they retire. With a doctor's salary, I can buy a nice house, and they'll live on the first floor."

Here Kiran did a perfect Indian accent, the words all singsong: "'*Kiran-beti*, you are such a good daughter.' Did I mention that I can only date Punjabi guys?"

She explained that her parents expected her to be at the "ultranerdy" University of Chicago in the fall because she could commute from home. Kiran wanted to go to Michigan, to be a normal college girl who lives in the dorms and goes tailgating on Saturdays.

Wow, I thought, *it's so rough to have your tuition paid for at one of the best schools in the world. I'd kill to go to the University of Chicago.* But someone in this room had made it impossible for me.

"Wait," Kiran said. "I lied. I mean, that's not the worst. I lied about coming here. They think I'm in Haiti, vaccinating poor kids. They think it'll look good for med school."

"Whoa," said Whitney.

"Well, well, well." Kat tapped her fingernails against her glass. "The plot thickens."

I didn't know Kiran had it in her.

"So what would your parents do if they found out?" asked Whitney.

"Cut me off financially. Or better yet, disown me like my cousin Neela," Kiran replied matter-of-factly. "She wanted to marry her white boyfriend. My aunt and uncle haven't spoken to her in five years."

I had little sympathy. Kiran had parents who loved her so much they wanted her to be successful in one of the best universities anywhere. And they wanted to maintain their shared culture. It didn't seem so unreasonable to me.

"That's harsh," said Whitney.

Kat's contribution was simply groaning. "Parents are such fascist dictators."

I was unconvinced that Kat understood the meaning of "fascist."

Kiran turned to me. "Nessa? Your worst thing?"

"I stole medication from the nursing home," I said. "A bottle of Xanax with six pills left. Barely worth talking about."

"Did we drink all the brandy?" Kat asked. "You guys sound like you have regret. Well, maybe not Nessa. But *regret* is why you consider these things the worst you've ever done."

Kat continued: "It's all relative. Some people might think what I've done is bad, but obviously I don't. So I 'had relations' with a married guy, but I've never kept it a secret. I'm not the one who took vows. That's on him. I don't regret a single orgasm. How about this? In Paris, no regrets."

"Really?" I asked. "That's the worst thing you've ever done? You didn't cheat?"

"We were never exclusive."

I couldn't believe that she refused to confess. Or worse, she didn't think what she'd done was wrong.

"I see. You're such a good person. So *unique*." I willed myself to stop—this wasn't the right time to remind her of those cheesy affirmations. Just a hint that I might know something.

And then Whitney undermined everything.

"Kat," she said, "I dare you to seduce that mime we saw today."

Kat smiled. "The one in the park behind Notre-Dame? Of course."

"Go back to the square," Whitney said. "And fuck a French mime."

"How'll we know she did it?" I asked. I was furious at Whitney for wasting a challenge Kat would've done anyway.

"Take his beret or something," Kiran suggested.

"Why would I lie?" said Kat.

Plenty of reasons, I thought.

When I found out that I was pregnant after a drunken encounter, I vowed to take full responsibility for that mistake. A lesser mistake than the one I'd made before, but a life-changing one. I promised that I'd make things right. I hoped, desperately, for a little boy. And I'd name him Vincent.

When the sonographer told me I'd be having a girl, I wept with grief. My obstetrician thought they were tears of joy. I don't blame him—I was a good actress by that point.

Because Vince's heart condition was possibly genetic, the doctor ordered an echocardiogram. But my heart was perfectly normal in terms of anatomy (even if a bit dark). My little Cricket's is normal, too (I make her go to a cardiologist annually).

Two years later, I met my husband. He's loving, generous, and kind, an excellent adoptive father to Cricket. Sometimes I think he indulges her too much. I don't want her to be the type of teenage girl who hates her mother. No, that's inaccurate—I don't want her to have to be a teenage girl at all.

Kat had returned that night with the mime's black beret in hand. But she was dejected because the mime had turned out to be Russian or Ukrainian, not authentically French. Groggy and exhausted, we asked if he was any good. She told us that he wasn't bad, but it had been difficult to do it standing up in the defunct elevator of the apartment lobby. I hadn't really considered the logistics of it when Whitney challenged her to the dare. I was tired and didn't have the momentum of the game—I'd have to start over in the morning.

It was only 8:00 p.m. Paris time, but we were jet-lagged and decided to go to bed. True to form, Kat stole all the covers from the bed we shared under the kitchen alcove, our sleeping arrangements decided via rock-paper-scissors. She'd taken everything from me—and now the blankets, too. It was absurd. Although it was early June, I had to close the kitchen window from the chill.

I crept into the living room. Kiran and Whitney were fast asleep on their striped cushions—Kiran curled into a fetal position with a blanket around her head, Whitney on her back, wheezing softly. Earlier that afternoon, I'd looked out the living room window and noticed a wooden pallet made for plants. There was enough ambient light and no window screen. I could fit on the pallet. And I had a pack of Marlboro Lights with my name on it.

I returned to the kitchen to find that book of matches in the cupboard. Then I tiptoed into the living room, matches and smokes in my hand, and tried to crawl out the window. The sill creaked as I put both knees on it. I looked back, expecting to wake Whit and Kiran, but neither of them moved.

I made my way onto the pallet and folded my legs, Indian-style. After freeing the pack of Marlboros from their cellophane prison, I plucked out a cigarette and put it between my lips. I struck the match along the black line and, with the snap of my wrist, saw the flame manifest. I inhaled a little to make it catch, just as Kat had instructed Whitney to do when we were at Notre-Dame.

The end of the cigarette glowed, which I considered a success. I took a deeper breath, letting the sharp smoke fill my lungs. I didn't cough, as I'd expected, but felt a jolt of adrenaline, my heart pounding in my chest.

A few of the surrounding apartments were illuminated, but blinds or curtains obscured their occupants. Across the courtyard, an unadorned kitchen window flooded with light. A young woman with dark hair pulled into a chignon, maybe thirty years old, placed a white vegetable on a cutting board and began to chop. I couldn't tell what it was—an onion? An endive or shallot, fancy vegetables I'd heard of but had never seen in real life?

Then a man appeared and kissed the back of her neck softly, just below her chignon. She shivered and laughed before turning to him. I imagined the couple would pour glasses of red wine and talk about their day. I decided that the woman had had the day off (she was an audiologist), but he was an academic and had spent the day working on his dissertation. He was excited to share his discovery with her, a new letter purportedly written by Shakespeare.

The man left the kitchen abruptly. The woman picked up the knife and rubbed her eyes with the back of her hand. Was she crying from chopping the onion or about something he'd said?

I didn't know why I bothered being curious about their lives. I tried to blow smoke rings, to no avail. I stuck my tongue out as I exhaled, assuming that would do the trick. Not so much. I'd managed to ace the ACT, but I couldn't figure out how to blow a smoke ring. I laughed at myself, both an act of self-deprecation and all-out defeat. Kat had bested me.

The man came back, kissing that same spot at the woman's nape and wrapping his arms around her from behind. They stood like that for a few moments, until she put the knife down and returned his embrace.

Just outside the apartment, pigeons cooed in the morning light. While I waited for the other girls to wake up, I was considering how to express my pain in a suicide note. Maybe if others felt a fraction of the anguish I did, people would understand my leap from the Eiffel Tower. Suicide wasn't tragic—it was a release. And a new beginning, one that would include my beloved brother.

I was disappointed Vince hadn't visited me that night. I'd had no dreams at all. Soon, though, I'd get to see him again.

I'd written several drafts of the note, but none fully conveyed my suffering, so I'd scrapped them. Better to leave a bit of mystery anyway. It wasn't as though people would ever get it, even with the most articulate suicide missive. The unknown was more interesting to the public anyway.

I tried to wait patiently as my travel companions went about their morning rituals: showering, primping, and coffee drinking. Plus, bitching about the Louvre and Musée d'Orsay being closed. I was annoyed—time was of the essence. We were in Paris, for God's sake.

Whitney wrinkled her nose as she smelled the dark liquid in her mug. "This is *definitely* not French vanilla."

"No?" I said, mostly to fill the space and keep Whitney from having a tantrum. I was flipping through the guidebook—I'd memorized sections on the Île de la Cité, the Latin Quarter, the Eiffel Tower, and Père Lachaise.

"When do you think the workers at the Louvre and Orsay will break the strike?" asked Kiran.

"How should I know?" I snapped, already regretting my words. Kiran wasn't the source of my frustration. "Sorry. That came out wrong."

"The Orsay museum has tons of Degas," Whitney said. "He's my absolute favorite. The ballerinas are so elegant."

"Degas was a pedophile," I said, flipping the page.

"Let me guess." Whitney narrowed her eyes and cocked her head, ready to fling an insult. "You read that in your private genius library."

"Actually, no. Just think about it," I said. "He always painted—and sculpted—prepubescent girls."

"So true," said Kat, emerging from the bathroom perfectly coiffed. "Your turn, Whit."

"Thanks," Whitney said. "Espècially to you, Eeyore. Degas is *not* a pedophile!"

I was secretly pleased. I'd never had a nickname before. It seemed that the three of us had made an implicit pact not to mention Whitney's hair. She was still beautiful. I didn't understand why Whitney had made such a fuss.

Once, before school, I'd put my hair in curlers and carefully applied the drugstore makeup I'd borrowed from one of the nursing home ladies—I did eventually return everything to her. I wanted, more than anything, to be noticed. I'd been so sick of being invisible. In first period, I sat down in my psychology class, in the second row, as usual. From behind, I heard the most popular girl in school, Aimee von Allsburg, ask who the new girl was. I turned.

"Oh, it's just Vanessa Baxter," she said, with an air of distaste.

Just. I'd been noticed, like a shiny silver earring on the ground, only to be discarded when the earring turned out to be a familiar foil gum wrapper. I hated the way that she, like so many others, used my full name, as they did with all of the school outcasts: Ellen Steiner. Zachary Coates. Vanessa Baxter.

Of course, I still wanted to be noticed. Jumping from the Eiffel Tower was a statement the world couldn't ignore. While I'd scrapped the suicide note, I had several glossy senior photos in my messenger bag that I figured would be found and used in the newspapers. I'd spent most of the money I'd earned working in the Pine Haven cafeteria on good pictures. The flattering portrait made me look like a normal high school girl, my big smile revealing straight, pearly teeth (I could thank my father for the nice teeth and complexion). I wore the letterpress *V* pendant that Vince had given me. It appeared as though my biggest problems were deciding which lip gloss to use and wondering whether we'd beat the Panthers at homecoming. I imagined the photo printed in newspapers all over the globe, the grin at odds with my untimely demise. People would ask: *Why?*

As I waited for my travel companions to be ready for public consumption, I busied myself by reading about more sights of Paris, like the sex museum Kat had talked about. I was somewhat disappointed to find no actual photos of the Erotic Museum, only blurbs for discerning readers. The collection held "every manner of sexual art, from well-endowed stone talismans to Victorian pornography."

Finally, the other girls were ready, and we headed down the apartment stairs and into the obnoxiously sunny morning. I was glad the other girls had taken the "L" back home in Chicago. I knew that I could figure out public transportation, but I'd never actually used it before.

The metro station smelled of piss and cigarette smoke. Still, it did have a certain charm, with its art deco entrance and green tile. I followed the girls' lead by buying my ticket and swiping it through the turnstile. Of course Kat, the glutton, was the first to spot a vending machine on our platform and remind us we hadn't eaten breakfast. She bought a bunch of Belgian waffle cookies and passed them around.

I hadn't had much of an appetite since puking up the Nutella crêpes, and it was further suppressed as I watched a pigeon on the tracks picking the bones of what looked to have been, at one time, a rat. The bird's head bobbed in and out of the carcass's rib cage.

Soak it all in, ladies, I thought. *Our first morning in Paris.*

"That may be the most disgusting thing I've ever seen," Whitney said, nodding toward the pigeon.

"Circle of life," I noted.

I was ridiculously pleased with this unexpected little gem. When we stepped on the train, I tried to look as bored as the other passengers (and keep my balance as we lurched forward). When we got off at Barbès-Rochechouart, we were immediately accosted by Arab men hawking metro tickets or Marlboros. We had to keep shaking our heads no while looking straight ahead. By the time we reached the street, the goods had changed to boxes of perfume and cologne. I'd memorized the map of this arrondissement but still had the guidebook in my messenger bag, just in case.

We'd entered another world, one with women dressed in head-to-toe black burqas walking around scraps of trash littering the sidewalk. I smelled sweat, roasting lamb, and rotting garbage. I was positively gleeful to see my companions' pained expressions.

"There's the flagship store?" Whitney pointed to the corner. "Whoa. Ghetto with a capital *G*."

Signs screamed "Tati" in bright-pink lettering. Bins of tchotchkes and boxes of clothes spilled onto the sidewalk, promising deals for anyone willing to dig. Women in dark headscarves, balancing infants on their hips, sorted through the mess.

"*That's* the famous Tati? Seriously?" Kat said. "We'll hit it after the museum and Montmartre. Then we won't have to carry around bags all day."

Leave it to Kat to make a decision for all of us. I led them along the boulevard, passing several low-rent bridal shops and kebab places before the street gave way to XXX stores and peep shows.

"I don't think we'll find cute party outfits at Ghetto-R-Us," said Whitney. "This is like a huge deal. Our girl's going to lose her V-card, but the outfit has to be perfect."

"Yeah, we have to get your cherry popped," added Kat.

"Relinquish your maidenhead." I remembered that term from *Romeo and Juliet*.

"Nice," said Kat, elbowing me in the side.

I backed away from her touch as if burned. She didn't have my permission.

"It can't be that bad," said Kiran. "Right?"

I didn't know if she was referring to the store or having sex for the first time. In a feat of extraordinary timing, we all noticed the old Frenchman in a fedora walking beside us, his hand deep in his own pants. He grinned.

"*Quatre jolies filles,*" he said, as if he couldn't believe his good fortune. "*Quatre!*"

He said four pretty girls, not three. Believe it or not, he was including me.

S ince that fateful trip, I've spent a lot of time learning how to reconcile reality with expectation. For example, I didn't expect to see the outline of her broken body under the sheet, her left hand and wrist twisted unnaturally, palm toward the sky in surrender. It looked nothing like the beautiful corpses of Cleopatra or the martyrs. It's amazing how we fool ourselves into thinking death might be pretty, that we still have the power of beauty after our demise.

There's a painting in the Louvre, *The Young Martyr*, by Delaroche, that I'd wanted to see. It depicts a blonde girl with a halo, floating in dark water, her wrists bound and head thrown back in either agony or ecstasy. A fine line, no? I remember reading somewhere that the neurons responsible for pleasure also register pain. *La petite mort*. It's about expectation versus reality.

I've tried to compartmentalize everything and hide it under layers, glossing over the irritating grain of sand like an oyster making a pearl. It hasn't worked. I still see her picture, the one they printed all over the news. And then, just a few years ago, when an Italian schoolgirl tried to jump from the tower, her photo was all over the news again and went viral online. This time, it was a reminder of the tragedy and her martyrdom. My friend didn't die in vain, because after her death, the French government installed safety mesh that saved the Italian schoolgirl, Chiara something or other. I found the YouTube video of the Italian mother praising Jesus to be a bit much.

Chiara was also beautiful. What other power does a teenage girl have?

The girls had been disgusted by the old guy who'd stared at us while jacking off, but they seemed less fazed than I'd expected. They all seemed eager to find the Musée de l'Érotisme, which was tucked between two sketchy lingerie shops.

"Old dudes," said Whitney, catching a singed strand that had fallen from her barrette. "They're the worst. Dirty old men."

"I prefer to think that people over fifty don't have sex," Kat said.

"What exactly encompasses a sex museum?" asked Kiran.

"Talismans," I replied. "Historical pornography."

The window display housed an old wooden chair with a wheel of rotating tongues where one's crotch, if sitting in the chair, would be tickled. Otherwise, it resembled a perfectly normal dining table chair.

"Nice," Kat said. "I cannot *wait*."

"I know," said Whitney. "Cause you're a . . ."

Kiran looked at me, as if deciding whether to intervene and smooth over the situation. She was the only one who had yet to undertake a dare. I was trying to figure out how to incorporate the museum—it was a delicate situation. Her dare had to be light-hearted, so she'd keep playing with us, but enough of a challenge that she didn't think we were treating her differently.

"Say it," barked Kat to Whitney. "Finish your sentence."

"Oh come on," said Whitney. "You're proud of it, you little slut."

"No, I'm a *big* slut. Thank Christ and his donkey," Kat said, making the sign of the cross.

I found her little dig at Whitney's Catholicism amusing. After paying the admission fee, we decided to start on the first floor and make our way upward. The first floor housed the gift shop, which featured a curated selection of sex toys, but most of the space was dedicated to cabinets displaying phalluses from around the world. The origins of the dildos were identified with somber placards in both French and English.

I was both intrigued and revolted by the selection of phalluses—I didn't expect so many primitive, rough-hewn wooden ones from Africa and Asia. There were also carvings of fucking couples interspersed throughout, and even one of two horses mating right beside a horny couple.

"Hey, Kat," yelled Whitney. "I've got one big enough for you!"

We all migrated over to Whitney's discovery. It was a giant, whale-sized wooden dildo from Indonesia.

Kat's eyes widened. "Holy shit."

"That's like the size of my *leg*," Kiran said, holding up her calf for comparison.

I became distracted by the strange devil masks to my left. I was drawn to the darkest visage. Up close, I could see the mouth was actually made of two naked women folded into grinning lips. I didn't like that sex was symbolized as evil, but I did like the complexity, the darkness and the light. My mission was to keep showing my travel companions more of the darkness, the pigeon eating the rat carcass—in other words, real life.

"We need a good dare for you," I said to Kiran.

"No," Kat said, issuing a direct challenge to my statement. "This place is too sacred. We have to respect the institution."

I couldn't think of an articulate way to debunk her messed-up logic.

"Are you, like, hearing yourself right now, Kat? What, are you chicken?" Whitney asked, and started clucking. "Or should I say a scaredy-Kat?"

"As if," said Kat. "You didn't even complete your dare. You didn't actually light the cigarette."

"Whatever," Whitney said, conceding that round.

Knowing the others would probably follow, I started up the marble stairs. The marble was the same gray as Vince's urn, which made me sad, as if I were somehow stepping on him.

He was larger in death than in life, just as I would soon be. The school had had a memorial in the gymnasium with all of the students and nearly three hundred people from town. As a three-sport varsity athlete, he'd always been popular. Vince was tall, tan, and gregarious. Obviously, he had his pick of girls. But he was also a normal teenage boy—he wasn't perfect. Once I'd heard him call Zachary Coates, the kid with cerebral palsy, a retard. Not to his face, but in passing with friends: "Come on, guys, retarded people have feelings, too."

Vince always ate my raspberry Yoplait in the fridge, even when I labeled it with my name in Magic Marker. I usually ended up doing his laundry, and once when I was searching for rogue socks, I found a porn magazine that showed women tied up with leather straps. Still, I loved him fiercely—he was my brother.

When he died, he became a saint. Everyone had a story about his kindness. They talked about how he'd rescued a kitten from a drainpipe, but they left out that he was allergic, and the poor thing had feline leukemia anyway, so the vet had to euthanize it. They remembered how he'd taken Ellen "Stinky" Steiner to the prom, but I knew it had been for a bet with his buddies Jake and Ben. To Vince's credit, he'd refused to take their money.

At the memorial, girls wept over him. Not just crocodile tears, but Kleenex-clutching, bleary-eyed sobbing. A few of the boys, too, though they were less conspicuous about their grief. Even Coach Gilbert cried through his eulogy, his big paw of a hand scratching at his eyes as though he had an insatiable itch. I'd sat there on the bleachers, numb, until I realized that I didn't have to stay there. I was the dead boy's sister, a celebrity in my own right. So I just got up and walked away.

On my way out, I hadn't been prepared for the makeshift memorial along the chain-link fence surrounding the track and football field. People had stuck flowers and baseball caps and teddy bears in the fence, not to mention the photos and newspaper clippings.

The posters, made with construction paper and Magic Marker, proclaimed "We Love Vince" and "R.I.P. #34." The grass in front of the fence was littered with candles and even more flowers, many of them carnations in the school colors, burgundy and gold.

To die young was to be immortal, to leave more questions than answers. Wasn't that what we all wanted? Some people dreamed they were extraordinary, and when they realized that they weren't, they had kids in order to leave a legacy. But I could do better than just getting knocked up. Anyone could do that. I would shout, look at the absurdity of our existence! I would end the sentence of my life with an exclamation point that demanded attention! Because I would leap from the world's most visited monument! And it would be as easy as jumping off the dock into Werners' pond.

The pink monkey penis protruding from a 3-D painting on the landing brought me suddenly and irrevocably back to the Musée de l'Érotisme.

"Eww!" Whitney shrieked.

I took in the entire composition, which included a woman in a green dress with her lips on the monkey's penis. Whitney's reaction seemed both appropriate and somehow wholly inadequate. I just kept walking up the stairs. I could hear Kat saying something, but I was too far ahead to make out the words.

The second floor contained lots of cartoonish pornographic drawings. I wondered where all the classic female busts were until I realized those were probably considered high art, and I'd probably see them at the Louvre, if we made it there. Some of the drawings here were graphic enough to make me uncomfortable. The other girls were oohing and aahing over the sexual positions, and when Kat started giving Kiran advice, I made my way to the top floor.

There, I found a love seat in the shape of red lips and a TV. The screen showed an old black-and-white silent film. The guy had a killer Victorian mustache, all thick and curled upward at the ends. A woman in a nun's habit joined the couple just as I started to zone out, thinking about the next dare. What could I challenge Kiran to do that would maintain the delicate balance?

To my delight, on the other side of the room, I found a big art notebook that served as a guestbook. Other museum visitors had signed their names, along with the date and their nationality.

I scrawled "Vanessa Marie Baxter, USA," and drew a mini Eiffel Tower. I'd been practicing my sketches and was happy to find an appropriate forum for my morbid little joke. *C'est la vie.*

After our foray into the sex museum, we walked toward Montmartre, the hill of martyrs, and the frosted wedding cake of a church that was Sacré-Cœur. I could smell fresh popcorn. On the sidewalk, a toothless man in a djellaba twisted the metal handle of an old-fashioned popper. I wasn't surprised when Kat, with her insatiable appetite, bought two bags. Only after shoveling popcorn into her mouth by the handful did she offer the other bag to us.

The popcorn was light and fluffy, with just the right amount of salt. I found myself eating more of it than I expected. Beside me, Kiran practiced throwing a kernel in the air and catching it with her tongue. A few of the women in headscarves shot her dirty looks. She grinned back at them. *Good for her,* I thought. *Baby steps.*

Whitney got lost window-shopping, admiring the cheap bridal shops we were passing.

"Hey," she said. "Let's go look. Just like five minutes, okay?"

I'd never gone to prom—I was never asked, even as part of a bet—but I did like the formal gowns in the windows. I already had a basic black outfit for my jump, but I was thinking maybe I should do it in style, in something elegant yet dramatic. I had a credit card, cosigned by my mom, for emergencies. Surely this could be considered an emergency. It's not like I'd ever have to pay off the debt. And it wouldn't be a financial hardship for her, since she'd never have to pay for me again.

Whitney cooed over the middle dress in the window, a satin gown with white floral embroidery cascading down the skirt.

"Oh my God, that's my dress. It's so perfect. I'm, like, so serious right now," said Whitney, pressing her fingertips to the glass. "When I get married, I want to be wearing, like, that exact piece of heaven."

"I prefer this one," Kat said, pointing to the pale gold one on the end, her mouth still full of popcorn.

"But that's a bridesmaid's dress," Whitney protested.

"Plain white's way too boring and conventional," said Kat.

I found this funny, considering Kat always wore a white button-down shirt.

"I like white," Kiran chimed in.

"Kir-bear," Kat said, chomping on the last of the popcorn, "I dare you to try on the ugliest dress in the store."

"For real?" Kiran asked. "Do you think they'll let me?"

"Confidence," said Kat. "Own it."

It took me a while to understand Kat's end game. As we entered the store, a young woman with black hair and vampish lipstick greeted us. I noticed that she'd failed to blend the scarlet outline of her lip pencil with her black cherry lipstick, creating a two-tone effect.

"Bonjour," Kat said to the lipstick girl.

The brown carpet was stained in random spots, and I noted several kernels of popcorn ground into the floor. While we set about scanning the racks for the most hideous dress we could find, Kat chatted with the salesgirl. She reverted to English and said her friend was getting married. I wasn't sure how much the salesgirl understood.

The prize for ugliest dress ended up being a tie between my pick and Whitney's: a two-piece lace gown with three-quarter sleeves on the bolero jacket, found by me; and a frothy satin cupcake of a dress with billowing medieval sleeves, discovered by Whitney. They were both exceedingly ugly, but Kiran went with Whitney's choice, possibly because it was so huge that it could stand up on its own. I still didn't understand the stakes of this dare.

Kat asked if they had the dress in Kiran's size. The girl went to the back for a few minutes, returned with the gown in a smaller size—not that it seemed any smaller, given the amount of fabric of the design—and helped Kiran into the dressing room, which was really just a corner of the store with a sliding curtain. The salesgirl unzipped the dress for Kiran to step into it and then retreated.

I could hear rustling satin, and Kiran said from behind the curtain: "Somebody zip me up?"

Whitney went in to assist. Finally, Kiran emerged and stopped in front of the three-way mirror. Kat did a wolf whistle, and the salesgirl said, pandering to my French stereotypes, *"Oh là là."* But poor Kiran looked like a young pine tree weighted down by two feet of snow.

"Yeah," Kiran agreed. "That's definitely it. Good find, Whitney."

She twirled around in front of the mirrors, making the skirt billow like a white parachute—or a white flag of surrender. Her smile fell into a frown, and then a grimace. The tears burst from her scrunched-up face.

"It's not that ugly," Whitney said with a nervous laugh. "You know that you can still wear white, even if you decide to have sex. Right?"

"But I can never have this," cried Kiran. "Even this awful thing. I have to wear a red sari and marry some random Punjabi engineer."

I stood, paralyzed. I didn't know how to comfort a weeping girl—I couldn't even comfort myself.

"Hey now. I thought it might be good, you know, wearing the ugliest dress. No crying in Paris, remember?" said Kat, lowering her voice to a whisper. "Whitney, go distract the salesgirl, okay?"

Whitney did as she was told, probably out of loyalty to Kiran.

"Here, take this," Kat whispered, pressing the mini Swiss Army key chain into Kiran's hand. "Now go back in there and cut it off. Rip that ugly thing from your gorgeous body."

"That's part two of the dare," I added, as if that were the plan all along.

As Kiran pulled back the curtain and set to work, Kat asked if we were ready to run. I reminded her that running would look suspicious, so we should simply walk faster than normal. Kat conceded that I was right.

When Kiran came out in her regular clothes, we all hustled out of the store, Whitney bidding adieu to the salesgirl.

"We did some future bride a favor," said Kat.

"We saved a wedding," added Whitney.

I kept looking over my shoulder, hoping we might get caught. I figured a brush with the law might be beneficial for them. It seemed that they'd never been held accountable for their actions, and I wanted to see that happen sooner rather than later.

When I was pregnant with Cricket, I took an adult and pediatric CPR class. Even before we were allowed to touch the adult plastic torso at our knees, we had to shout, "Annie, Annie, are you okay?"

We had to assume no response, that Annie was most certainly not okay. She was made of peach-colored plastic, sported an androgynous haircut (made of the same peach plastic), and wore a dark-red zip-up jacket, the sleeves hanging limp because she had no arms. After I'd pressed my lips to hers and practiced mouth-to-mouth resuscitation, I had to wonder who she was and why she was called Annie. That high forehead, those softly closed eyes, the lips slightly upturned in a partial smile—she was mysterious.

An Internet search revealed some information: in the 1950s, a Scandinavian toymaker was asked to make a prototype for a rescue doll. But he was stumped about how to create the face. It was agreed that a female would be more approachable, so he sought the perfect visage for a victim, to no avail. While visiting his grandparents, he noticed a beautiful plaster mask hanging on the wall. The toymaker stole the mask and modeled the rescue doll after this lovely, serene face, the final countenance of an unclaimed girl who'd been found in the Seine.

And why was her death mask hanging on the wall in the first place? In the morgue, a French pathologist had smoothed clay onto her face and made the first of many plaster molds that would eventually be displayed as decoration. Throughout late nineteenth-century Europe, young women of the day held up her beauty as the ideal. The face of a dead girl. Rumors of her demise abounded. There were no marks on her body, so she likely threw herself into the river.

Before the updated Red Cross guidelines, which no longer require mouth-to-mouth, Annie was the most kissed girl in the world. Because Cricket completed a first-aid course when she was twelve, I know the training now only requires chest compressions, performed at one hundred beats per minute to the Bee Gees' song "Stayin' Alive."

I still think about that damn manikin and wonder why we aren't teaching Annie how to save herself.

I didn't get my wish—it seemed that we could get away with anything, including destroying a wedding gown. Nobody was looking for us. Kiran insisted that we didn't have anything to worry about, which made us suspicious.

"Um, okay," said Kat. "Where's the Swiss Army knife?"

Kiran hesitated. We had to weave around a group of Algerian mothers with infants hoisted on their hips. One of the babies reached for Whitney's golden hair as she passed.

"Right here. I couldn't do it, okay?" said Kiran. "The dare was to try on the dress, not ruin it."

"I totally respect that," Whitney said, giving her unsolicited opinion. "I mean, weddings are so beautiful, seeing two people declare their love. Maybe that's some girl's dream dress."

"Says the wannabe wedding planner." Kat was now enjoying a cigarette.

"Just because you're, like, so cynical doesn't mean everyone should be," countered Whitney.

"Touché," I said.

"Nessa, speak English. Time for the ghetto department store?" Whitney asked.

Despite Tati's tacky exterior, with overflowing bins of sale merchandise and people digging through them to find bargains, the clothing inside was chic and affordable. I followed the girls around as they squealed and said things like, "Oh my God, look at this top!" and "This is tragic. They don't have my size in this one."

I wondered what each of their lives would be like. Whitney would probably be a good event planner, thoroughly invested in the satisfaction of her guests and the popularity of her parties. Kiran would be a great doctor, even if she hated the thought that her parents were right. As for Kat, who knew? I didn't understand how she could possibly cheat her way through Yale. She'd be good at white-collar crime. She'd also have nightmares about my jump and have her therapist on speed dial. Her actions would catch up with her eventually.

Once each of the girls had an armful of clothing, plastic hangers clacking, I followed them to the dressing rooms. We had to pass through the lingerie section, with lots of sheer lace, the bras and panties so skimpy that I wondered why French women bothered with underwear at all.

"Ness, you have to try something on," insisted Whitney.

"Everything's pretty, um"—here Kiran paused—"affordable. And nice."

So Kiran pitied me. At least she was aware my family didn't have money. I knew the girls would keep harassing me until I joined them, so I grabbed the nearest item of clothing, which happened to be a red lace bra and matching thong. The smallest sizes they had.

"Excellent choice," said Kat.

I wanted to punch her.

What happened next was a strange ritual of both deprecation and praise. I had seen the trope on TV and in movies, but never in the wild. It boiled down to each of the girls stepping out of a dressing room, barefoot and shorter without their sandals or shoes, and saying some variation of "I hate my [body part]. [Other girl]: I wish I had your great [body part]." Another girl would say: "Are you kidding? I'd kill to have your [other body part]."

I was peeking through the door of my dressing room to get an overview of the situation. Eventually they'd make me come out. I chastised myself for not having the foresight to find something more innocuous. The sexy red lingerie was a far cry from my usual soft white bra and cotton Hanes underwear.

The focus, at the moment, was on Kiran. She wore a leopard-print spaghetti-strap tank top and black boot-cut pants.

Whitney squealed. "That's it! That's the outfit that'll make you lose your virginity!"

"Hot," said Kat. "Turn around. Kiran, you have a great ass. Now you just need some fuck-me heels."

I'd only seen Kiran in jeans and T-shirts—she looked stunning.

"Nessa," Kiran said. "Are you ever coming out?"

I took a deep breath and opened the door without stepping forward. Kat whistled. I slammed the door shut.

"But you look totally sexy," Whitney said.

"Yeah," said Kiran. *"Oh là là."*

Through the louvered door, I blurted the first thing that came to mind: "Wearing the color red attracts guys because it signals fertility."

"Then we'll all get matching red lingerie," said Kat.

"Les Sœurs Rouges." That had to be Kiran's voice—the Red Sisters.

I was flattered and humbled by their responses. It was as though they actually liked me.

I ended up using my emergency Visa for the bra and thong, which the other girls also bought. For outfits, Kiran got the leopard-print tank and black pants, and black platform heels. Whitney decided on both a shimmery blue tube top that matched her eyes and a black tank (in case she changed her mind) with a gray miniskirt. Kat, deviating from her usual black and white, purchased a silver sequin halter top and strappy platforms.

Les Sœurs Rouges. I couldn't imagine they were welcoming me into their fold. Were they?

In Montmartre, we decided to climb up the winding cobblestone streets and have lunch in the Place du Tertre, a square full of portrait artists and gullible tourists. The restaurant was overpriced and the waitress automatically gave us menus in English. But she was friendly and attentive, and she'd given us a table outside.

Kat, as usual, ordered the most extravagant things on the menu, mussels in white wine sauce and grilled baby squid.

Whitney objected. "Squid?"

"You know calamari is squid, right?" said Kat. "The fried deliciousness at Italian restaurants?"

"Yes." Whitney rolled her eyes, although it was obvious that she hadn't known. She ordered a *salade*, lamenting her metabolism.

I ordered the roast chicken, and Kiran got a ham omelet with *pommes frites*, again disregarding her past vegetarianism.

"Meat!" said Kat. "I bet Anton will show you a nice piece of ham tonight."

"You're making it sound so romantic," Whitney said.

"Just trying to keep it real."

"So," Kiran said. "It's gonna hurt a ton, right?" She took a drink of the water we'd ordered, *plat*, because we didn't like the sparkling, or *eau gazeuse*.

"Not necessarily," said Kat. "Lube—lots of it. Lube is your best friend. We'll get some on our way back to the metro."

"It helps to be a little tipsy," said Whitney. "So much easier to relax."

Kat unrolled her napkin and placed her silverware to the side. "Nessa, you're usually a fountain of information. Don't you have anything to add?"

"Nope. My first time wasn't good. Speaking of virgins, do we have to go to Sacré-Cœur?" I hoped my diversion tactic would work.

"Wait," said Whitney. "What does the Sacré-Cœur have to do with virgins?"

"Mary. Jesus," I said. "The saints. All virgins."

"I think I'm on cathedral overload after yesterday," said Kat. "Another time?"

"I know this is horrible to say," mentioned Kiran, "but churches all kind of look the same to me. Aren't we going to Père Lachaise?"

Finally, I thought, *someone remembered.* I was starting to have a soft spot for Kiran.

Our waitress brought another bottle of Evian. Just as she turned her back, a stooped old woman with ratty silver hair approached the table.

"Fortune?" She wore a dark shawl, despite the heat.

"Go away," said Kat, flicking her hand. "Shoo!"

"Cheap," the old woman said. I counted only three teeth in her entire mouth.

"*No.* Go away."

The old woman shook a curled index finger at us. "Die. One of you."

"Hate to break it to you, but we're all going to die," Kat said. "And pay taxes. Now leave us alone."

The woman moved on to the table next to us, a family who sounded German.

"Okay," Whitney said. "That was creepy."

"She just said that to get some money from us."

But the gypsy was right. I smiled and suppressed my laughter. She was so accurate that I wanted to give her a few francs.

Finally, our food arrived. We must've all been famished, because the conversation died for a while. Kiran ate the ham omelet with gusto.

Whitney finished her meal first. "We need a better dare for Katrine here. I think she enjoyed her random guy too much."

"Patience, grasshopper," I said.

Kat laughed. "He wasn't random. He just wasn't French."

I then argued that Père Lachaise was off-limits—if the sex museum was too sacred, then a cemetery with the remains of famous people was, too. Kat shrugged. Kiran and Whitney agreed.

"Fine," Kat said. "Whit, you didn't actually light the cigarette, which was the dare. So I dare you to cut off all your hair. It's singed anyway."

Whitney's hand went immediately to her barrette, as if to make sure it was still there.

"You could get a pixie cut," said Kiran brightly.

I had to admit—the idea was brilliant. But I was loath to have Kat usurp my position as mastermind.

"Remember when Brad and Gwyneth had the same 'do? You'll look just like Gwyneth in *Sliding Doors*," said Kat.

"That was such a good movie," Whitney admitted. "Probably my second favorite, after *Pretty Woman*."

Even Kat's manipulation was spot-on. Whitney looked nothing like Gwyneth—she had a heart-shaped face with rounded cheeks still plump with the last of her baby fat, and a little button nose. Her silky blonde hair and blue eyes were the only similarities.

"Okay," Whitney said. "But I want to get my portrait sketched first." She nodded toward the artists in the square.

We paid the bill and set out to find the best artist, based on the sample portraits they displayed. Whitney chose one who drew his subjects in a more realistic, less idealized manner. He had shaggy, sand-colored hair and blond stubble, and smoked his cigarette from a long, thin black holder, à la Cruella de Vil.

Whitney sat in a wooden folding chair in front of his easel. He stared at her for some time—I didn't know how he could see with his hair in his eyes—before making a series of rounded lines on his large sketchpad. Then he stopped, squinted at Whitney, and made a few more swipes of charcoal on the paper. He repeated this process several times.

I folded my arms, rocking back and forth on my heels. I was impatient to see Père Lachaise, which I expected to be the highlight of my trip. I reached into my messenger bag to assure myself that I still had my glossy portraits for the newspapers as well as Kat's affirmation notecards.

"Voilà!"

Finally, the artist was done. He turned the easel to show Whitney his handiwork.

"Merci," she said, giving him a fake smile.

He sprayed a fixer on the charcoal and rolled the portrait into a tube. She thanked him again. But as we walked away, Whitney asked, "Do I really look like that?"

It was a fair question. We all hoped that we were perceived as being better than how we felt inside.

As we walked back to the metro through the sketchy Pigalle neighborhood, I spotted a low-rent salon with headshots of women from magazines Scotch-taped to the window.

"That place appears to give haircuts," I told the girls.

"I double dare you," Kat said to Whitney.

"I'm going to look like Gwyneth," said Whitney. "And you're all going to be so jealous."

She strode into the salon and we followed. A middle-aged woman with cheekbones like cut glass greeted us. Kiran tried to interpret the elaborate progression of hand gestures made by Whitney and the stylist. I didn't know exactly the haircut they were talking about, so it seemed pointless to try and translate. Whitney finally pointed to one of the magazine cutouts taped to the wall.

The stylist motioned for Whitney to sit in a salon chair and whipped out a black smock, which settled around Whitney like a dark tent.

The woman said something about being certain, her face skeptical. I moved closer to hear.

"Are you sure?" asked Kiran.

"Yeah, I'm sure," said Whitney. "This is for real. The big leagues for the big girls. Like, how many times do I have to say it?"

"She was just repeating what the hairdresser asked," I snapped.

The stylist lifted hair from the back of Whitney's head, the woman's index and middle fingers pointed upward about four inches from Whitney's scalp. Then she made a scissoring motion with the other hand.

"Yes," said Whitney, exasperated. *"Oui!"*

The stylist took real scissors from the countertop and cut, a clump of golden tresses falling to the floor like a tassel from a graduation cap. More blonde tassels fell each time the blades came together. Snip, snip.

"As exciting as this is," said Kat, "there's a sex shop next door. Come on, Kiran, let's get you some Astroglide."

With that, I was alone with Whitney and the stylist. What on earth would we talk about? I scanned the rows of nail polish along the far wall, a rainbow contained in little bottles. I didn't know why anyone would care to paint her toenails fungus green, but it appeared to be an option.

"You should get a haircut, too, Ness," said Whitney. "Nothing drastic, just some layers like Jennifer Love Hewitt."

The stylist was snipping away. I settled into the empty barber chair next to them. "You can put lipstick on a pig, but it's still a pig."

"Oh, shut up, Eeyore. You're so gorgeous that people think you're *French*. What's your deal?" Whitney asked.

My lips parted, but I had nothing to say. My throat pinched and my tongue felt too big for my mouth. As I tried to swallow, the corners of my eyes stung. To keep from crying, I bit the inside of my lip until I tasted salty, metallic blood.

No one had ever said that to me. Not even Vince. He just said that I'd be pretty when I was older.

Suddenly I felt shame, a deep sense of failure, for linking my appearance with my self-worth. I hated that, as girls, we were constantly being judged for how we looked. But I was so flattered by Whitney's compliment that I had almost wept. Why should my looks even matter to me? They shouldn't, but they did.

"Thank you, Whitney," I eventually said.

"From now on, every time you're a downer, a puppy dies," she said. "Do you want to be a puppy murderer?"

I laughed despite myself. "Of course not. Who doesn't love puppies?"

"Yeah, don't be a killer." Whitney smiled and looked up at her new bangs. "It's a little shorter than I expected."

The stylist appeared to be finishing—at its longest, around Whitney's forehead, her hair was about three inches in length. It was difficult to imagine a more fitting (or horrible) punishment for her. With Whitney's petite stature, she resembled a twelve-year-old boy. I couldn't decide whether to tell her the truth or lie to save her feelings. But I didn't have to do either, because Kat and Kiran had returned.

"Whoa," said Kat.

I was so caught up in my own drama, fretting about my looks and Whitney's unexpected kindness, that I hadn't seen them come in.

"I think it looks cute," Kiran piped.

"Peter Pan, what have you done with our friend Whitney?" said Kat. "Are you holding her hostage in Neverland?"

Kiran elbowed Kat, which made it even more obvious that Kat's rhetorical questions were both inappropriate and perhaps too honest.

"Suck my Peter Pan little dick, beeyotch," said Whitney, her blue eyes hardened and her jaw tight. "I refuse to give you the satisfaction of crying."

"But crying always satisfies me. Really turns me on." Kat did that annoying thing where she arched an eyebrow like a cartoon villainess.

"By the way, I am *not* paying for this." Whitney brushed a few cut hairs from her shirt. "Don't forget the tip."

"Sure thing," said Kat, whipping out a silver MasterCard. "It's on Daddy."

Oh, how different our lives were.

On our way out, as the stylist was sweeping up the last of the blonde hair, I snagged a tassel and put it in one of the small front pockets of my messenger bag.

At long last, we'd gotten on the metro and disembarked at the conveniently named Père Lachaise stop. The neighborhood couldn't have been more different from Pigalle—the boulevard was eerily quiet and subdued, lined with funeral statuary places and floral shops. The summer sun created a glare on the windows. A couple of vendors sold magazines and maps of the cemetery. The graveyard was just across the street, fortified by a thick wall of stone.

"People need maps for a graveyard?" Kat asked. "Just point me to Jim Morrison."

"It's more than a hundred acres." I knew plenty of trivia—famous residents included Oscar Wilde, Chopin, Balzac, Molière, Édith Piaf, and Sarah Bernhardt, among others. Père Lachaise was first created when the Cemetery of the Innocents collapsed into the surrounding neighborhood, spilling the bones and corpses of millions of Parisians. Originally called the Cemetery of the East, on what was then the outskirts of the city, it had a marketing problem: no one wanted to be buried there. So administrators transferred the remains of Heloise and Abelard, ill-fated medieval lovers, as well as playwright Molière and author La Fontaine. The ploy worked, and it became fashionable to be buried there.

I also knew that for interment, the deceased must have lived or died in Paris. Family tombs usually contained many remains stacked on top of each other. Since the cemetery was owned by the city, families had to maintain their own plots. Groundskeepers only took care of communal spaces.

"We should get flowers," said Whitney. She kept combing her new bangs with her fingers, compulsively sweeping them to the side.

"For whom?" I asked.

"For *Jim.*"

Was I supposed to have known this? We stopped at one of the stands, where Whitney chose a bouquet of deep fuchsia roses. I bought two postcards—one of the Eiffel Tower and one of Père Lachaise, because I couldn't decide which one to send my mother as a good-bye. Kat bought more cigarettes, some French Gitanes, to leave on Jim's grave. I had a fondness for the Doors' music, but this seemed extreme, especially given all the great writers, composers, and artists in repose.

We crossed the street and trotted up the stairs to find a lovely city of the dead. Narrow stone chapels the size of phone booths marked the graves like little houses for the departed souls.

"Yo, Encyclopedia Brown," said Kat.

You used the encyclopedia when you needed it, I thought, reaching into my bag for those stupid notecards. But now wasn't the time—I had to wait until I was alone with her.

"Walk up the Avenue de la Chapelle a ways," I said. "And hang a right when you see the crowd."

"How'd you—"

"I know everything. Meet back here in an hour?"

They agreed, fortunately, so I could be alone with my thoughts. The cemetery was indeed beautiful, the sunlight filtering through the chestnut and plane trees, illuminating the cobblestone path and kissing the peaked stone chapels. I wanted to rest here for eternity. And why couldn't I? I would die in Paris, so I had burial rights. Maybe a well-meaning group of Parisians would make donations for the plot and associated costs.

I sat down next to an elaborate tomb with a statue of a weeping Greek woman, bent over the headstone with grief. I pulled the cemetery postcard from my bag and wrote my note on the back: *Please bury me in Père Lachaise. It is my dying wish.* And signed it simply, "V." I secured it in one of the smaller pockets so that I wouldn't lose it, but also so someone could eventually find it when I was gone.

I stood, feeling energized, and continued down the path, because I wanted to see the authors' graves. I wondered if the plots along the main avenues were more expensive. Surely the more visible areas were coveted. The monuments became more varied as I walked up the hill—neo-Gothic, neoclassical, even obelisks and pyramids.

An older woman was arranging fresh daisies on a shiny granite slab, with window cleaner and a dish towel at her side. Many of the graves had fresh flowers, though some had sun-faded artificial flowers or long-dead bouquets. I was surprised the French went for any tacky artifice.

I found the tombs with human statues, especially with the deceased lying down with hands in prayer position, to be particularly creepy. I liked the monuments that looked like little houses, with elaborate doors and decorative stained-glass windows. A few had grates, and I peered inside. There was just enough room for a mourner to stand or kneel, if she so desired. But the mini mausoleums were padlocked.

The newer graves were covered by flat granite slabs, and a few of them displayed small photos of the deceased on their headstones. I kept doing the math in my head, scanning the tombs for girls my age. The first I found was Daphne Thibert, 1948–1966. As I was searching for more girls who died at age eighteen, I saw a man with round spectacles sitting by a grave, reading *Le Monde* aloud. The headstone read "Marie Clair Giroux, 1930–1998." The other side read "Claude Giroux, 1928–" without the year of his death. *Oh, poor Claude,* I thought. Reading the news to his recently departed wife.

I didn't believe love like that existed. In movies, maybe, or novels, but not in real life. Of course, it was fleeting. Even if I found such affection in a devoted husband like Claude, he would die, and according to population statistics, most likely before me. So I could try, and possibly even find fulfillment for a while, but it would end in a brutal and traumatic way—no matter what. If he didn't leave me like my father left my mother.

I came upon another young woman's grave, this one with the same birth year: Sylvie Martin, 1981–1999. I plucked a lily from the bunch and tucked the blossom behind my ear. Despite the warmth of the day, the lily felt ice-cold against my skin.

I noticed the occasional forgotten grave, the crumbled stone ravaged by time and weather. We would all be forgotten eventually. But to die young, at one's peak, was to capture the world's attention—look at Jim Morrison.

I stopped at another abandoned grave. A young tree flourished, rising from the center of the tomb, one of its roots resembling a skeletal arm, as though reaching from the underworld.

At Père Lachaise, the sky became overcast, with pewter storm clouds rolling overhead. I hadn't thought to bring an umbrella or a jacket. I'd planned everything else so carefully, but I'd neglected to check something as simple as the weather forecast.

A couple of backpackers milled around a tall stone covered in scribbles and lipstick kisses. I gravitated toward it: Oscar Wilde.

I loved the art deco angel flying from the tomb. It had an actual penis instead of a neutered Ken-doll bump. I stood back and read the inscription:

And alien tears will fill for him
Pity's long-broken urn,
For his mourners will be outcast men,
And outcasts always mourn.

Alien tears, indeed. I couldn't remember if he'd killed himself or died of some nineteenth-century scourge like consumption.

"Want some lipstick?"

I was startled by Kat's presence. She was alone, standing beside me, twisting a tube of bright-crimson lipstick.

"Didn't know you were a fan of his," I said.

"My father was cast in *The Importance of Being Earnest* at Yale," she said. "Apparently it was a big deal, since he wasn't a drama major. Whenever it's playing anywhere in metro Chicago, he drags me with him to see it."

I chose my words carefully. "Are you excited about New Haven?"

Kat shrugged. "I'm excited about the amazing pizza at Sal's."

This was my moment. I foresaw the confrontation going one of two ways: either Kat would continue to deny any wrongdoing, or she'd somehow try to justify her actions. I figured it would be the latter.

"Tell me. How exactly are you going to cheat your way through college?"

Kat didn't answer—instead, she tucked the lipstick back in her purse. She got out a pack of Marlboros and tapped the end to retrieve a cigarette. She put it in her mouth and lit it, cupping her other hand around the flame so the breeze wouldn't blow it out.

Answer me, damn it, I thought. I pulled the notecards from my bag. "You think you can get away with it because you're 'unique and worthy of love'? Or because you're 'intelligent and capable of great things'?"

Kat blew several smoke rings, staring at the flying angel.

I couldn't stop reading the cards. "Wait, I know. It's because you're 'beautiful inside and out,' right?"

"You stole those," she said simply.

"You stole my whole fucking life."

"What are you even talking about?" Kat asked, picking a fleck of tobacco from her tongue.

"Are you seriously going to pretend like it never happened?" My voice was thick with venom.

"You mean the ACTs," Kat said. "Come off it—the whole thing was a win-win situation. You got to quantifiably demonstrate your brilliance, and I got into Yale. Wouldn't want to disappoint Daddy dearest. He practically had a stroke when I was in middle school and too stupid for algebra."

"I'm just collateral damage to you?" That bitch was so numb and calculating that she was incapable of empathy.

"I don't understand the problem," said Kat. "With a perfect score, I'm sure you got in everywhere."

"Oh, fuck you in your cold, dark heart. My scores were *cancelled*. There wasn't enough time to take it again before the scholarship deadlines. And are you really naïve enough to think I could ace it twice?"

She swallowed, holding her eyes shut for a couple of moments longer than a blink. "I didn't know they cancelled your scores."

"Of course you didn't. You were dealing with your horrible rich-people problems." A fleck of my spittle landed on her cheek. She didn't wipe it away.

"Not being a Yalie would be a failure," Kat said. "My dad gave me Yale socks. Socks! Like, multiple pairs. We go to New Haven once a year on pilgrimage. Our white bulldog is named Handsome Dan."

"Am I supposed to understand that reference?"

Kat had shrunk, visibly, and I realized that I was at least four inches taller than she was. She had only loomed large in my imagination.

"Mascot. Yale Bulldogs," she said, her voice cracking. She snuffed out the cigarette with her sandal. "I didn't want to break his heart."

"But it was okay to break mine."

"What do you want from me?" Kat asked. "To admit that I'm dumb? That I'm not smart enough to get good grades on my own?"

Was I supposed to forgive her ignorance? Tell her everything was fine? After all, my life was still ruined. Nothing could change my mind—I'd still implement my plan at the Eiffel Tower.

"It's true," she continued, and lit up another cigarette. "I cheated my way through high school. I'm flipping my shit about college because you're exactly right. I have no idea what I'm going to do. I should probably just go to the University of Chicago and take all my classes with Kiran like I did at Wash."

"What's up, bitch?" said Whitney, with Kiran in tow.

Above us, the sky rumbled with thunder. The air became gray and sullen. I wondered if French thunderstorms were like midwestern storms, where the air felt so thick that it gripped your throat until suddenly the pressure let up and the heavens split open.

"How much did you hear?" asked Kat.

"Most of it," replied Kiran. "Jesus, Kat, you could've just asked for my help. You're my friend. Or so I thought."

"So you cheated off us," Whitney said.

"Well, not off you, brain trust." Kat blew smoke into Whitney's face, making her cough.

"Why are you such a *cunt*?" Whitney said.

"What're you going to do?" Kat said. "Shave off my eyebrows?"

"How *are* you going to cheat your way through Yale?" Kiran folded her arms across her chest.

"Are you deaf? I said I don't know. But Yale will be filled with smart kids. And I'm a damn good actress—I won't get caught again."

The temperature had dropped nearly ten degrees, and the gray clouds spit drops of water upon us. Kiran had had the foresight to bring an umbrella, but it was a small folding one and barely covered her, let alone three of us. Kat was excluded for obvious reasons. Then one of the metal tentacles broke, spilling water onto me and Whitney.

Kat started running ahead of us, holding her Tati bag over her head as she ran. Her white shirt was already soaked through, revealing a beige bra—the back of it, anyway. She stopped abruptly, in front of a narrow chapel, and waved back: "Come on! This one's open."

Despite the fact that Kat was now hated by the entire group for varying reasons, none of us wanted to be standing in the pouring rain. I was freezing. So we squeezed inside the phone-booth-sized space with our fair share of profanity and jostling. It smelled like a musty basement. I stood on my tiptoes to take up less room, the cool stone at my back, but as fate would have it, I was facing my enemy. The physical irritation of having her body so close to mine was countered by the warmth that I desperately needed.

I keep waiting for the other shoe to drop. Other parents, mothers especially, warned me about teenage daughters. Girls are so sweet, until suddenly one day they hate you. They are cruel and seethe with contempt. This, of course, I know too well. I have no doubt that her fury will erupt, leaving me to choke on the ash.

Yet that day hasn't come. Cricket is still quick to laugh and find silver linings. She has a large circle of friends, most of them swim teammates, and goes to all of the school dances. She receives a lot of text messages from a boy named Alex, but she insists he's not her boyfriend because she "doesn't have time for that."

Who is this angelic creature, and how could she have possibly come from me?

We were all silent on the metro ride back to our apartment. I was perplexed—I couldn't decide if I hated Kat more or less now that I knew she'd been unaware of my cancelled scores. Why hadn't she noticed, when everyone else was talking about college, that I hadn't said a word? And once, at a French Club meeting, when Kiran had asked where I was headed in the fall, I just shrugged and said, "I'm not sure that I can afford everything." It seemed like a failure of empathy on Kat's part. A colossal failure of empathy. She couldn't see outside herself.

In any case, I hoped to be important and adored in death, just like young women throughout history. Despite my gawkiness, I was strangely photogenic, and that's what people would remember: a pretty girl who perished at her own hand. Like Ophelia, sliding down a willow tree into a stream, surrounded by flowers. I hoped to see another painting in the Louvre, by Delacroix, that depicted her death. But I wasn't sure that I'd make it to the Louvre. It didn't matter much, so long as the Eiffel Tower workers weren't on strike.

As we were walking up the stairs from our metro stop, Whitney finally broke the silence. "So are we going back to get ready for the party?"

"Yes," said Kiran.

And so it was decided. It was refreshing to have Kiran calling the shots. Kat, for her part, didn't object. All of her power was gone.

Wet and cold, I started peeling off my soaked clothes the second we entered the apartment. For the first time, I wasn't self-conscious about my skinny body. What did I care, given that I was going to fling it from the Eiffel Tower? I changed into the black tank top and pants that I'd packed.

The other girls used Whitney's blow-dryer to dry the outfits they'd purchased at Tati. Whitney offered it to Kiran first, then used it herself, and finally left the thing in the living room, at which point Kat was allowed to use it. The new hierarchy had been established.

They spent the next hour bobbing in and out of the bathroom, primping and prepping. I was amused at the lengths they went to in order to impress Anton, Luc, and their friends. We'd known these guys for all of forty-five minutes, the amount of time for the van ride from de Gaulle to central Paris.

When I wasn't observing the girls' elaborate beauty preparations, I was sitting on the carnival-stripe cushions, reading the "suggested day trips" chapter of the guidebook. I learned that Marie Antoinette's favorite place was the bucolic Queen's Hamlet in the gardens of Versailles and that the colors of Disneyland Paris were more subdued than its American counterparts, owing to European tastes.

"Eeyore," sang Whitney, "have you killed any puppies since our chat?"

"Only a few."

"Can I do your hair? Please, please?" Whitney asked.

I didn't see any harm. "Sure, knock yourself out."

"Yay!" She clapped her hands.

I was amazed how easy it was for her to experience happiness. And all I had to do was say yes.

"Okay, you stay right there," Whitney said.

"Aye aye, captain."

She returned with an arsenal: a curling iron, outlet adapter, round brush, hair spray, and an aerosol can of something I couldn't identify. My mom had never been one for hairstyling. Her "style" was always wash-and-go, usually pulled back in a ponytail or a simple braid. I had adopted the same look, largely by default. Since my hair was dark and stick-straight like my father's, I could shower and run a comb through it—my hair would dry perfectly straight.

"You ready for this?" Whitney asked.

"Ready as I'll ever be."

"This is going to look so awesome. Okay. Mousse first." She shook the aerosol can and pressed on the top to produce a palm full of foam. Then she rubbed both hands to distribute the mousse and gently applied it to my hair, starting with my scalp. I relished the touch of her fingertips. It was rare that anyone deliberately touched me—I was grateful and happy that Whitney wanted to do so.

Beginning at the back, she took a section of hair and clamped it with the curling iron. Whitney ran the iron down to the ends and flipped them under with a twist of her wrist. I could feel the heat at the base of my neck. Whitney held it for at least thirty seconds before moving on to the next section.

"Maybe you'll meet someone at the party," she said.

"Maybe," I said, "but I doubt it."

"Puppy!" Whitney cried. "A puppy is dead. An adorable little pug puppy."

"Fine." I smiled. "Maybe I'll meet an awesome guy and have mind-blowing sex."

Whitney lowered her voice so it couldn't be heard in the kitchen alcove, where Kat was sitting, or the bathroom, where Kiran was primping. "You're a virgin, too, aren't you?"

My first impulse was to be defensive: never give a girl information that could be used against you. "No. I slept with Adam. At summer camp last year."

"What camp?" she asked, now at my left side, curling under the sections there.

"Camp, uh," I started. Now I was cornered. "Camp Wishaponna."

Whitney laughed so hard that she had to unclamp my hair. "Nessa, you're going to make me burn your neck with this thing. It's nothing to be ashamed of, you know."

"Camp Wishaponna sounds like a place for cancer kids, doesn't it?" I said. It was actually pretty funny.

"Totally. You use tampons?"

"Yeah?" I didn't know where she was going with this line of inquiry.

"The super kind? And it doesn't hurt to put them in?" Whitney pulled a chunk of hair in front of my face and flicked the ends under with the curling iron. "Did you bike a lot as a kid or ride horses?"

"I rode my bike all the time with my brother. I didn't know super-absorbency tampons were supposed to hurt." The thought of being an equestrian, from a working-class family, was absurd.

"Oh, they're not. That's like, a good thing," Whitney said. "It means that you don't have a hymen and losing your virginity may not hurt."

"That's . . . good?"

"That's *awesome*."

Kiran came into the living room in her new outfit, the leopard-print top and black pants. She'd blow-dried her hair straight. It was a far cry from her usual tomboy athletic look—I hardly recognized her.

"Your hair looks so pretty!" Kiran cried.

"Kir-bear, you look amazing," said Whitney. "All that and a bag of Doritos."

I murmured agreement.

"Thanks," she said. "But I can't get my eyeliner right. Can you help me?"

"I'm almost done," replied Whitney. She'd loaned out her makeup to Kiran.

I'd always been a decent draftsman, and I could certainly draw a straight line, so I offered. "I can try."

To my amazement, Kiran sat down in front of me and handed me the charcoal eyeliner pencil. The three of us were like an assembly line of primping. I started with Kiran's right eye, pulling her closed eyelid to the side and gliding the pencil along her lash line. Then I did her other eye.

"Perfect," I said. And meant it.

B efore I go to bed, I peek into Cricket's room, just as I've done for years, and look for the familiar rise and fall of her chest. I set my alarm for ten minutes earlier than usual so I can braid her hair like I used to when she was little. She gets up at 4:30 a.m. for morning swim practice, and I always make her breakfast.

Today she wants eggs over medium, the whites firm but the yolks runny so she can dip her toast in them. As she sits at the kitchen island eating, I ask if I can French braid her hair.

"Sure, Mom," she says, as if she understands my nostalgia. "But it's just going to get covered by my swim cap."

I grab a brush from the bathroom and set to work. I love to feel the wavy black strands between my fingers. The muscle memory kicks in, and my hands move deftly, weaving sections of extra hair into the braid, just like a mother at the playground had taught me to do ages ago, and I'm finished before I have much time to savor the moment.

I didn't want Cricket to become a teenager, but it happened, despite my resistance. I even refused to buy her training bras and only relented when I saw the straps from a bra she'd borrowed from a friend. When she came home from a sleepover wearing lipstick and eyeliner, I ordered her to wash it off and sent her to her room until dinner, mostly so I could weep in private.

Kat entered the living room, where we'd been getting ready for Anton and Luc's soirée. None of us looked at her.

"You know," she said, "you're going to have to talk to me eventually."

Whitney turned to me and Kiran. "I don't think we need to interact with the bitch who betrayed us, do we?"

"Nope," Kiran replied.

"Well, for starters," said Kat, "I have the directions to the party."

I combed my memory, hoping to recall the specifics. "It's in Belleville, I know that."

"You don't remember the address?" Whitney whispered.

"Cut me some slack," I hissed. "I didn't know it'd be necessary to memorize that information."

"I propose a temporary cease-fire," announced Kat. "Let's just get drunk and have a good time."

If we wanted to attend the party, we had to acquiesce. And I had to be around Kat to encourage her participation in Truth or Dare and implement my ultimate plan.

"What about the game?" I said. "I still need my second dare."

"Me, too," said Kiran.

"Okay," Whitney said, "but you're no longer queen bitch, Kat. You, like, don't get to dictate anymore."

"Your wish is my command."

"We'll believe it when we see it," said Kiran, the sharpness of her voice jarring me.

"Would you ladies like to take a cab?" Kat asked, without sarcasm or malice. "I saw them out today. They must not be on strike anymore."

The three of us looked for the others' approval, giving slight nods. It was agreed. I didn't think anyone, myself included, wanted to see another decaying rat corpse. One dose of reality was enough.

"So what should we bring?" asked Kiran.

"Depends," Whitney said. "Do you think it'll be, like, really elegant? I can totally see everyone drinking wine and smoking cigarettes and listening to jazz."

In our burgeoning democracy, I felt compelled to make an offering. "Why don't we bring some red wine? Something inexpensive but not too cheap?"

"May I suggest a young Côtes du Rhône?" said Kat. "They're reasonably priced."

Of course Kat would know such things. I remembered that her house had a special temperature-controlled closet in the basement—a wine cellar.

"Excellent," said Kiran. "There's a wine shop just across the bridge. Get us two bottles, please."

Kat hesitated for a moment, as if waiting to see if Kiran was serious.

"Run along." I made a walking motion with my index and middle fingers.

"Chop-chop," Whitney said.

Kat got her purse and left, just as we'd commanded.

Kiran giggled. "This is fun."

"Way fun," agreed Whitney.

"We should mess with her some more," I suggested.

"We could put a sign on her back," said Kiran. "At the party."

Whitney laughed. "Like a kick-me sign?"

I, too, was touched by Kiran's naïveté.

"Not exactly," she countered. "I was thinking one that said 'SLUT' in capital letters."

"Whoa," said Whitney. "Okay."

The depth of Kiran's anger only reinforced my own—the three of us were sisters in arms. Kat had several victims, and she deserved to pay for what she had done.

B efore Kat returned with the bottles of Côtes du Rhône, I gave Kiran a piece of paper from my would-be suicide notebook. She had a pen and wrote "SLUT," using the whole sheet and reinforcing the letters by tracing over them several times. Kiran then folded the paper into a square and tucked it into her purse.

When Kat returned, Whitney asked if she was wearing the red bra and thong. Kat admitted that she was, at which point Whitney insisted that she change—she was undeserving of the Red Sisters. And further inspection would be necessary to gauge Kat's compliance, said Kiran.

Whitney then flicked the strap of my tank top to reveal the only black bra that I owned, in and of itself a subversive act, because I'd had to buy it on sale at the outlet mall. Both Whitney and Kiran told me to go change into the red lingerie. We were *les Sœurs Rouge*, and I had to show my loyalty by wearing red. I'd never been part of a group before, not like this. Were these girls actually my friends? The evidence for such a conclusion kept mounting.

Once it was determined that I was wearing the appropriate red undergarments (and Kat was not), we headed downstairs to catch a taxi. After the thunderstorm, the evening had cooled to a pleasant temperature. I stepped off the curb, my right arm raised, and within seconds a cab stopped for us. I was giddy with power I'd never experienced. Was this what it felt like to be a pretty girl? Someone visible rather than invisible?

The taxi was a silver Mercedes with leather seats. I'd never ridden in a European import, let alone a Mercedes. I couldn't help but be impressed. Kat, who drove a sleek BMW coupe, courtesy of her father, had the foresight to sit up front with the cabbie. She also gave him the address. The three Red Sisters sat in the back, enjoying the fact that we had a chauffeur.

"So what's on the agenda for tomorrow?" asked Kiran.

"Eiffel Tower?" I suggested, reminding myself that nothing had changed. Kat had been nice to me before cheating behind my back. I wouldn't be surprised if Whitney and Kiran suddenly turned on me.

"We should totally do the Eiffel Tower," Whitney said, "but in the afternoon. The morning's a wash. I mean, what if we end up staying over? Or if even just one of us stays over?"

"Permission to speak?" asked Kat from the front seat.

"Briefly," granted Kiran.

"I think this is a good plan," said Kat.

And then I realized it was a competition. Who would get Anton? Who would get Luc? The problem was that I didn't understand the rules. I'd never played this particular game before—I was simply happy to be included.

Night had fallen on the city and Paris looked magical, all twinkling and full of romantic possibility. In academic pursuits I'd never lost—I'd been valedictorian and aced the ACTs. But I wasn't practiced in the art of seduction.

I imagined the party would be a chic Parisian affair, with wine, conversation, and food. I knew they'd probably want to talk politics, so in my head I brushed up on current events: President Clinton had been acquitted in the impeachment hearings (the whole thing was ridiculous—Europeans had affairs all the time, including politicians) and the air strikes against Yugoslavia were either a) necessary, if the Parisians thought the Serbs were committing acts of genocide; or b) completely unwarranted, and yet another act of American aggression. The massacre at Columbine High School? Yes, absolutely, we should have more gun control. It would never happen in Europe, and with good reason.

The taxi finally stopped at our destination in Belleville. Kat paid the cabbie with cash. We looked up at the apartment building, which was more modern than any of the buildings near our rental. That didn't say much, given that so many of the buildings in central Paris were nineteenth-century constructs. Luc and Anton's building was only forty or so years old and maybe eight stories high, taller than most. Like American architecture of the time, it was boxy and functional.

"We can't go in yet," Whitney insisted. "It's only 10:15."

"Okay," said Kat, setting down the bag with both bottles of wine. "When are we allowed?"

"When we've each had a cigarette." Whitney snapped her fingers twice.

Kat, playing her new role of assistant, gave a Marlboro Light to everyone and handed off the lighter. Since I'd practiced before, on the rooftop, I was confident I could pass this test with flying colors. I lit mine and took a long drag, as if to demonstrate my proficiency. Whitney was successful in igniting her cigarette, unlike in Notre-Dame. Even Kiran puffed on one, though she did cough a couple of times.

The street lamp glowed above us. I watched a moth fluttering toward the light. I imagined the sizzle of its wings as it collided with its would-be sun.

"So Kir-bear," Whitney said, "you ready for the big night?"

Kiran looked down but smiled. "Maybe."

Whitney then glanced at me, not saying a word. My secret seemed to be safe.

"Here," Kat said, producing a condom from her purse and handing it to Kiran. "He should have one, but you never know. You don't want to lose your V-card but get herpes or something."

"You know, I did pay attention in sex ed," teased Kiran.

"And you have the lube?" Kat asked, her voice filled with maternal concern, as if she were making sure her daughter had her stocking cap.

Kiran picked up on this, too. "Right here, Amma."

By this point I wanted to just go to the party. Maybe be the center of attention with my extensive knowledge of current events. But despite what I'd told Whitney, I wasn't hopeful. I couldn't overlook years of being ignored.

"Nympho, teach me how to blow smoke rings," Kiran commanded.

Kat launched into a tutorial. I think she enjoyed imparting knowledge—she just didn't have much to give.

"Okay," she said. "Put the tip of your tongue at the roots of your bottom teeth. Then purse your lips into an O shape."

She waited for Kiran to follow the directions. Without making a conscious decision, I found myself following along.

"Now do a really short exhale, like you're trying to clear the back of your throat. Like this." Kat demonstrated with a brief, guttural puff.

Kiran mimicked her, as did I. The trick worked. We were both blowing circles of smoke that floated languidly in the night air. It was like an adult version of playing with bubbles. So maybe Kat knew a few things.

"Good!" she said. "You can try to catch each other's rings."

Whitney flicked the gray worm of ash from her cigarette. "So Nessa, do you think Luc's hot?"

"I don't know." Revealing such information had hurt me in the past. Then I realized she was giving me an opening to claim him. And I'd just ruined my chance.

"Hot? He's beautiful," said Kat. "He looks like an Abercrombie model."

"You've gotta loosen up," said Whitney. "Have some fun."

My cheeks burned. She was trying to help me.

"It's your turn for a dare, right?" asked Kat. "I dare you to take whatever's offered to you at the party—weed, coke, X—whatever."

"Sure." I almost choked as I exhaled. She'd hit me at my most vulnerable—she knew that I couldn't let myself lose control, but if I took something at the party, I was more likely to do so. I knew that weed was marijuana and coke was cocaine, but I wasn't entirely sure what "ex" was.

"Wait, I almost forgot," said Kiran. "To show your penance, you have to wear this sign on your back all night."

"What's it say?" asked Kat.

"You're not privy to that information."

"Fine," said Kat. "Not like I'm afraid."

Kiran had even brought tape, and she set about fastening the "SLUT" sign to Kat's back.

I, for one, was afraid of what I might do if I lost control. Funny how I felt fully prepared for any offer of politics. Mind-altering substances terrified me, but I hoped that our political situation was more likely to surface than, say, pot or any harder drugs. We'd have boozy, somewhat contrarian conversations about Clinton's policies, and that would be the extent of it. We were in erudite, glamorous Paris, which, for all my cynicism, I couldn't deny.

I just read in the *Tribune* about promising research on unortho-dox treatments for post-traumatic stress disorder, including psychedelics and MDMA, the active ingredient in ecstasy. I will admit to using substances besides Klonopin over the years. I met a colleague's wife at a holiday party, a no-nonsense social worker named Janelle who deals with Chicago's child and family services. With all the horror she sees, I'm surprised she's not into harder drugs. Sometimes we take sick days together, for our mental health, and make mushroom tea. Usually we ingest at my house and then walk a few blocks to the lake, where we can watch the undulating waves and believe all is right with the world.

It was Janelle who told me about Molly, the unadulterated form of X that's all the rage with teens. I've never been good at elegant segues, so I simply wait until Cricket is home from swim practice and the team's carb-loading spaghetti dinner.

I rarely have to knock, because she generally keeps her bedroom door open. Her walls are covered in French paraphernalia—the tricolor flag, photographs of Montmartre by Brassaï, and the coupe de grâce: a giant canvas print of the Eiffel Tower. Daniel, of course, bought that for her. Édith Piaf warbles in the background. I'm convinced Cricket is the only girl in America to have memorized all of the Little Sparrow's songs. The room smells faintly of chlorine, as does Cricket's skin.

She's on the floor, foam-rolling her calves. The girl is always in motion, in the water and on land. When she isn't unconsciously tapping her feet, Cricket is gliding her fingers across her iPad or typing on her phone with her thumbs.

"What's this about Molly?" I ask. "Being very popular?"

"Molly Lieb?" Cricket says. "She's going down. Her splits aren't as tight this season, especially in the free and backstroke."

Oh, how I love this child more than life itself. While she's mature in many ways, she's blissfully naïve in others.

Her phone chimes. She stops rolling to check it.

"A boy?" I ask.

"It's Mikayla. Asking about the bio homework." She holds out the screen for me to see. The text box reads "#3b. Help?"

I exhale. I didn't realize that I was holding my breath.

"Mom," Cricket says. "I'm not having sex. I promise."

She's remarkably adept at interpreting my facial expressions, because she continues: "In the unlikely event that that changes, I know the pill is—wait for it—99 percent effective. Barrier methods are less effective, more like 80 percent. But obviously, hormonal birth control doesn't protect against STIs. The best approach is both. I *know*, Mom."

Good memory. That's my girl.

Once we'd all smoked our cigarettes, Whitney called up to Luc and Anton's apartment via the phone box in the lobby.

"Allo?" said a deep voice.

"Listen up, boys," Whitney said. "We've arrived, so the party can start now."

The front door buzzed open. We took a modern elevator up to what we assumed was the seventh floor, but all of the apartments were six-something.

"What the hell?" Our new leader, Whitney, was clearly perturbed.

"Oh yeah," said Kiran. "I bet they count the ground floor as the first floor."

"This is why they needed us to win both wars," said Kat.

I could imagine her father saying something like that. She was just an echo. I tried not to care, because Kat would get her just deserts. I had to admit that the "SLUT" sign on her back was ingenious. We ended up having to take a flight of stairs up to Anton and Luc's place, 7-G.

The door was propped open. Inside, several candles dripped wax onto a wicker coffee table, giving off the only light in the whole room. Books and dirty clothes were scattered pell-mell around the room. We followed the noise through the dark kitchen and onto a balcony the size of Kat's bathroom in her McMansion filled with guys our age or a little older. Inexplicably, most of them wore ripped clothing—was this a new trend? We were the only girls there. Open cans of beans and tuna and bottles of liquor were lined up on the ledge of the balcony, interspersed with the occasional flickering candle.

Beyond the ledge was a stunning view of Paris. The Eiffel Tower, in its twinkling glory, rose above the skyline. I hoped to find a quiet corner of the balcony to reflect upon its beauty, but given the current noise level, I doubted that was a possibility.

"*Bienvenue!* The Americans are here!" shouted a guy (Luc?) in camo pants, black military boots, a white ribbed tank top, and aviators. How did Luc see anything through those sunglasses? Then Anton approached, wearing a white robe and carrying a Bible, looking heavenly in the literal and figurative sense.

"What the fuck?" asked Kat. "I don't think we got the memo."

"It is the end of the world!" proclaimed Anton. His dark stubble had grown into a beard, thick and black, completely appropriate for a prophet.

"Ah, yes, more wine for kalimotxo," said a guy in medical scrubs and a flipped-up gas mask. He took one of the bottles of wine, deftly opened it with a corkscrew, and poured the entire thing into a half-empty two-liter bottle of Coca-Cola.

"That looks disgusting," said Whitney. "I mean, red wine and Coke?"

"I am Biel," he said, "as in Gabriel. And this is kalimotxo. Delicious! You will try."

While I was annoyed we hadn't been warned about the party's theme, I found the concept to be exquisite. It was almost too perfect.

"You didn't tell us there was a theme," said Whitney.

"No kidding," said Kat. "Might've been nice to know so we'd have costumes."

"We will fix this," Luc said, holding a pair of scissors in his hand. He grabbed at the side of Kat's sequin halter top—not that there was much extra fabric—and snipped before tearing a wide swath. He did the same for Whitney and then Kiran, who wouldn't stop giggling—she was nervous.

"You really should ask permission next time," Kat teased.

"Pants time." Luc tore the knees of her pants and along the left side of her inseam, stopping just a few inches from her crotch. *Yes,* I thought, *flaunt your body in the coyest way possible—make it look like you didn't mean to get naked.* God, she *was* a nympho. That's how she got all the attention. I turned, looking for other entertainment.

After performing a little bow, Biel handed me a cup of kalimotxo. It wasn't as bad as I'd expected. In fact, I found it refreshing. I made my way toward the ledge, weaving through several people, and planted myself in front of a jar of pickles. The tower glowed like a beacon: *come to me,* it said, *surrender.* It was then I noticed its searchlight sweeping over the city. *Better yet,* I thought, *find me.*

"I'd recommend the olives," said a freckled guy with a distinctly British accent, "but I'm afraid they're all gone. I'd avoid the canned hummus."

Not that I'd planned to eat any of the food. There were no utensils, just a number of opened cans. I supposed that, in the event of an apocalypse, silverware and manners would be of little importance.

"Duly noted," I said. "Where's your costume?"

"Same place as yours, love. I prefer to keep some of my dignity."

I swirled my drink, listening to the ice cubes pop. Ice seemed unlikely at the end of the world. "Where're you from? The Commonwealth?"

"Wales. Studying here for a year. I'm Owen." He offered his hand.

I couldn't decide if his sudden earnestness was endearing or irritating.

"I'm Vanessa," I said. "Nessa. American, obviously."

"Right, then. Did you bring a gun?" Owen asked. "For the apocalypse?"

Now I was paying attention. "What?"

"Luc tried to get one. His uncle lives in Marseilles, one of those wacko survivalists. Hoarding supplies and all for Y2K."

"So why are you asking me?"

Owen snorted. "Don't you Americans know all about guns?"

"Now that's just offensive," I said. "I don't know anything about guns, other than firearms are the top choice of American men looking to commit suicide."

"That's a lovely tidbit," he said. "On a lighter note, have you been to the top of the Eiffel Tower yet?"

"Soon," I told him. "You could say that I have an obsession with it. What do you want to know about the tower?"

I proceeded to rattle off trivia and stare at my beacon, its latticework illuminated by thousands of yellow lights, pulsing with the knowledge that I was dying to share.

Those facts are still burned into my brain. For example, I don't think I'll ever forget that Gustave Eiffel erected the tower in 1889 to commemorate the centennial of the storming of the Bastille. It also served as the centerpiece of the 1889 World's Fair, much to the chagrin of his fellow Parisians. Many felt it was an ugly eyesore. Some even called it "the Tower of Babel," a symbol of extreme hubris.

Gustave Eiffel was a mere five feet five inches tall. Interesting, then, that he created a giant tower made of iron latticework. Standing nine hundred eighty-four feet, or just over three hundred meters, it was the world's tallest structure until 1929, when the Chrysler Building was erected in New York City.

La tour Eiffel weighs seven thousand tons, but its weight is distributed over a base that spans two and a half acres. In a feat of modern engineering and elegant design, it sways no more than four and a half inches in heavy winds. It is made of eighteen thousand metal parts.

Parisians eventually acquiesced to its popularity and embraced it as a symbol of their beloved city. They discovered its utility as a radio antenna. During World War I, it was a significant addition to France's arsenal, aiding in the nation's victory. The Eiffel Tower is still used as a radio antenna and meteorological post.

Only one worker died during its construction, though he wasn't on the job. He was giving his paramour an advance tour when he slipped and fell. But his death was the first of many. In 1912, Franz Reichelt made a parachute, and in an experiment to test his design, jumped from the first level of the tower. The parachute failed.

In subsequent years, people leapt to their deaths without parachutes—only the overwhelming desire to leave this earth. I'd found a *TIME* article from 1966 estimating that 349 people had committed suicide there. The French government refused (and still refuses, for that matter) to release any official numbers.

I'd also discovered that in 1996, just three years before our fateful Paris trip, they'd installed more barriers to prevent potential suicides. Still, people on an Internet message board assured me that where there's a will, there's a way. It wasn't as easy to jump, but there were still places that would allow access if I climbed a few feet up a girder.

I'd learned all that I could before the trip, but in the end, my information didn't help me. Had I understood its potential for destruction, I would never have sought such knowledge.

In a cruel twist of irony, my little Cricket has wanted to see the Eiffel Tower since she was a very little girl. The very first *Madeline* book that my husband bought had the tower on the cover.

I have no doubt that he meant well, but it was the beginning of an obsession. In fourth grade, she wrote a report on *la tour Eiffel*. By sixth grade, she was studying French with a tutor. Lately she's been reading books and magazines in French to prepare herself for a trip. Just in case, she says.

I keep saying that we should start with Montreal—a much shorter flight and more manageable city. Maybe Paris when you're older, I tell her.

At the end-of-the-world party, I'd had enough liquid courage to be bold. The odd but delicious combination of red wine and Coke, which the Spanish guy Biel had some exotic name for, provided a nice, uplifting buzz. The candlelight and view over Paris were intoxicating.

Either Owen, the British exchange student, wanted to get inside my pants or he was waiting for something better to come along, because he was still talking to me. I don't think I'd ever spoken this long to a guy my age. It was thrilling—I felt witty and attractive. Then again, I had nothing to lose, so I'm sure my confidence stemmed from not really caring what he thought.

"It only took two years to build," I said, still educating him about my beloved monument.

"I haven't actually been yet," said Owen. "The French call it *la Dame de Fer*. The Iron Lady."

"Sounds like a torture device."

"I read that Eiffel didn't actually design it," he said. "One of the engineers in his firm did—one Maurice Koechlin. But the Koechlin Tower doesn't have the same ring, does it?"

This I had not known. In fact, it felt like a betrayal. The man I'd thought designed it, the diminutive Gustave, wasn't its original creator? Yet he'd taken credit? Sounded like Kat taking credit for my answers.

"Any other must-see places in the city?" I asked.

"The Catacombs," Owen said. "A bit spooky, but the patterns, the way the bones are arranged—very artistic."

Had I found a soul mate? Another morbid cynic? I assured myself that it was the booze intruding on my thoughts. On the other side of the balcony, I watched my three travel companions flirting. Anton, the beautiful false prophet in a white robe, had his arm around Kiran's waist, the Bible tucked inside his rope belt. Whitney was motioning with her cup toward Luc and his paramilitary garb. And Kat flashed a grin at Biel, the Spaniard in scrubs with a gas mask atop his head. It didn't appear we'd be leaving anytime soon.

"The French Resistance set up shop in the Catacombs," Owen continued. "The Nazis read the inscription that says, 'Stop! Here is the Empire of Death' and took it to heart. Never found the Resistance, which was literally underground. Lots of tunnels and caves under the city. I fancy myself an urban spelunker."

"Can I tell you a secret?" I asked.

"Sure." Owen pushed his glasses further up the bridge of his nose.

"I'm going to kill myself. See that girl over there—the one in the sequin halter top?"

Owen nodded solemnly.

"Well, before I do, I'm taking that bitch down."

He began to chuckle, which morphed into a full belly laugh. This was probably a reasonable reaction on his part, given what I'd just told him.

"You have such a dark European sense of humor," he said.

"I'm dead serious," I said, mildly amused by my own joke. "She ruined my entire life."

"I don't believe that you would take your own life, not for one minute."

"Oh? You don't think I have it in me?" I took another sip.

"Forgive me for stating the obvious, but someone so depressed as to be plotting suicide wouldn't have the fortitude for revenge," he said. "A truly depressed person doesn't have the mental energy to hate another person. Only herself."

"What are you," I said, "some kind of psychologist?"

"I'm studying psychology, yes."

He had just pulled at the loose thread, threatening to unravel the entire seam. One I'd worked so hard and meticulously to sew. I closed my eyes and pressed the cool drink to my forehead.

"So you've had a row with her," Owen said. "I assume you're just having a laugh, or it's a thing between your mates. The sign on her back and all."

"Yeah," I said, not wanting to make him suspicious. "Not funny?"

"Your mates look to be having fun." He gestured in their direction.

"Mmm, they've probably had more alcohol than us. Can I get you another drink?" This would be my chance to ditch him and pretend to talk to someone else.

"Nah, I'm more about expanding my consciousness, not limiting it," Owen said. He reached into his shirt pocket to reveal a handful of dried brown mushrooms. "Care to make the evening more interesting?"

As part of my dare, I'd promised to take anything that was offered. I didn't expect magic mushrooms to be part of the equation. I tried to remember facts about their effects from eighth-grade health class—I was fairly sure, but not certain, that they were mild psychedelics, and that you were less likely to have a bad trip using them than LSD. The latter bit of information was from Charlie Boyd, the class stoner, who'd chimed in at inappropriate times. Shrooms, he called them.

"Okay," I said. "But you have to tell my friends."

"I don't have enough for everybody, love."

"No, that's not what I meant. They think I'm"—here I searched for the right word—"square. No fun. But they don't know me very well."

"As you wish, love."

Owen then gave me five of the little mushrooms and told me to eat fast and chase them with Coke. *Bottom's up,* I thought.

Owen had warned me that the shrooms would need about thirty minutes to take full effect. The time passed like the slow drips of wax sliding down the candles in my peripheral vision. Eventually he suggested we go brag to my travel companions that I was lucky to be going on "an enlightened journey." He seemed nice enough, but it also seemed prudent to tell them about what we'd ingested, just in case he tried to pull something. The only person I'd allow to hurt me was myself.

As we looked to complete our mission, Owen got caught in conversation with Biel and some new guy. When I approached the girls, Kiran was whispering to Kat and Whitney. Anton and Luc were nowhere to be found.

"Hey," I said. "Where are your boyfriends?"

Kiran's expression gave me pause, as if I'd asked a painful question.

"Anton keeps calling her his 'Negro princess,'" Kat said. "Like it's 1930."

"Is that a bad thing?" I said. "Negro doesn't have the same connotations here."

"Luc was, like, literally slobbering on me," said Whitney.

I was confused—wasn't that the goal? They all wanted attention from Luc and (especially) Anton. How many hours had they spent primping and deciding what to wear? I wouldn't have been surprised if Kat was blowing this out of proportion because she wasn't used to being the third wheel. Biel seemed to be more interested in the other guys than Kat. "They're just flirting," I said. "It's the end of the world, remember? It's like we're the last people left on earth. Guys will say anything, you know."

Anton and Luc burst through the balcony door.

"The last vodka!" Luc proclaimed, holding the bottle high above his head. "A true apocalypse for Russia!"

Anton proceeded to pour the vodka into everyone's cups, whether we wanted it or not.

Suddenly, my head felt as though it were underwater. Sounds were blurry and pulsing, separating into individual notes. I heard only syllables, which I had to connect into words. So many syllables: *ee, ya, puh, kuh.* The mental work was taxing.

My hands and feet expanded and contracted with every beat of my heart. I felt the whoosh of blood after each contraction. My hands would grow twice their size for a moment, then go back to normal. Hearing the syllables of my name, I looked up to see all of the girls staring at me. Their eyeballs bulged so far from their sockets, I was afraid they'd pop out. I tried, desperately, to warn them of their impending blindness, but they didn't seem to understand. Why wouldn't they listen to me?

The mushrooms. Ah, yes, the expansion of consciousness that the British guy had promised. No, Welsh. *Same difference,* I thought. I told the girls, my Red Sisters, about the shrooms I'd taken and that I'd fulfilled my dare. Victory was mine! I was the first to successfully complete two dares, which seemed like cause for celebration. I won. I was a winner.

Their eyes continued to bulge. I worried that we should call an ambulance, but then I saw a doctor wearing bright-green scrubs and holding a respirator. *Help them!* I said. I told him about their eyes, but I didn't think it was contagious and assured him that he wouldn't need the respirator. I entrusted their care to the doctor.

The night sky flashed with pink light. And then I saw Him, my clandestine lover, who would embrace me and help me escape from this world. *La tour Eiffel,* in all His glory, glowed with a pink aura. I felt Him in the deepest recesses of my soul. This was my destiny. His pink light penetrated me. It was as though He'd opened a door to a room I had suspected existed but had never known with certainty. As I reached out to touch Him, I could see trails of light. Whenever I moved my hand, the glow followed in an extraordinary act of solidarity.

The entire city of Paris was breathing and pulsing with yellow light. The rooftops were beautiful, so exquisite in their symmetry that I felt the urge to weep. I had to share this knowledge.

I heard a voice say the syllables necessary for my name, and I linked them together in my head: Va-ness-uh. It was Owen, the Welsh psychologist. I thought he asked me if I liked the shrooms.

No, I like life. *I love the throbbing, choking, heartbreaking moments of this world! I am in love!*

Everything fell silent. I knew, on some level, the cognitive dissonance of what I said, what I felt, and what I knew. Then I pondered the three major theories of the twentieth century: relativity, quantum mechanics, and chaos.

Chaos theory. If the moth's wings flapping toward the street lamp here in Paris made a disturbance in atmospheric pressure, would it cause an earthquake in Indonesia? Chaos theory tried to explain seemingly random events. The normal heart had a variable rhythm based on complex factors, wholly unpredictable. But just before a heart attack, the beat was stable and followed a distinct pattern.

So profound, I thought. I was going down the rabbit hole, and I liked it. *I am Alice! I am in Wonderland!*

I knew that I was on a balcony with lots of other people, many of them wearing ripped clothes like zombies. The flame of the candle pulsated with happiness, the aura getting bigger and bigger with each pulse. To capture this happiness myself, I understood that I had to ingest it, make it one with my body.

As I was contemplating just how to do this, I leaned in and felt heat between my eyebrows.

And a miracle occurred: Vince pulled me back.

"Careful," he said. "You'll burn yourself."

He'd dyed his hair blondish and wore a torn flannel, which Vince would never wear, but I wasn't about to get hung up on the details.

I searched for the right words. "How do you like your new place?"

He told me it was nice and he planned to stay there for a while.

When I began to cry, he wrapped his arms around me, just like he used to do during thunderstorms at Werners' pond. When we were little, we'd ride our bikes out there and spend whole summers in the water.

Our mom took care of old Mr. and Mrs. Werner at the nursing home. While there was still a camping trailer parked on their property, it sat neglected. The rest of the Werner family rarely used the pond. When our dad wasn't working—which was rare—he would take us swimming there.

But usually it was just me and Vince, our lips purple from grape Kool-Aid and our skin brown from the sun. We'd take turns on the tire swing. Even then, he was athletic and could push me so hard that when I jumped from the tire, I was nearly to the middle of the pond. Our cannonballs were impressive. I loved that moment when I was launched into the air, just before I hit water.

We'd play great white shark, a game where one of us would swim with our hands in prayer position, just above our head, as a fin. We had to catch the person as soon as we could. Remarkably, in the water, I was just as fast as Vince. And while I was awkward on land, I was graceful in the water.

When we tired of these games, we'd circle the pond in a languid backstroke. We'd listen to the electric hum of the cicadas and look for shapes in the passing clouds. Beasts, usually, both domestic and exotic. If animal crackers had been on sale at the grocery store, our mom would buy us a canister, and we'd sit on the dock eating them. The first one to match a cracker with a cloud shape would win. The camels and bears were always popular, often winners.

Sometimes the clouds grew dark and ominous. I hated thunder. Vince loved storms, and if it were up to him, he'd probably have stood in the rain, arms spread. Instead, he'd put his arms around me, and we'd huddle under the cluster of trees.

"Don't worry," he'd say, tucking my wet hair behind my ear. "I'll keep you safe."

I came to realize that I hadn't been talking to Vince, and that I'd been speaking French to some random guy. The only option was to jump off the balcony, just like jumping into Werners' pond, and join Vince in his new place, wherever that was. Because I wasn't particularly coordinated, I was having a difficult time climbing the ledge.

"Vanessa, leave the dark place. Remember what makes you happy," said a voice. It was a remarkably coherent string of words. I didn't even have to put together the linguistic puzzle pieces. My happy place was Werners' pond, and I was trying to get there. But I couldn't do it. I remembered that deep love for life, my Alice moment.

I was confused. I found a familiar face in my field of vision. The Welsh guy, Owen, the one who'd said that I wasn't actually depressed, that I wasn't suicidal if I had the capacity to hate and plan revenge. I felt shaken and disoriented.

But I understood, somehow, that he could be right. I still wanted revenge, but I clung to the hope that I could not only endure but also thrive in the face of adversity. And I would.

Fucking Darwin. Fuck Darwin and his theory of evolution. Most of all, fuck how an individual member of a species scraped, clawed, and screamed to stay alive.

"Quite the journey, eh?" said Owen. "Here, drink this. The sugar will help your digestion."

He seemed experienced in this realm, so I drank the entire thing, opening my throat and letting the bubbles slide down.

"You want to see something amazing?" he asked. "It's not my dick, I promise."

His red hair was still glowing a little. It seemed like a reasonable proposition.

"It's a happy place," he said.

"Okay."

"Come on, love," Owen said. "Let's get a cab."

He took my hand and led me out of the apartment, but not before we heard bedsprings from behind a closed door.

"Somebody's having a good time, eh?"

"Definitely," I said.

We rode down in the elevator, which had several mirrors. For a brief moment, the echoing images felt like the tunnel of eternity. But then I could recognize the beauty and symmetry of fractals, the beauty of everything around me.

O wen led me down a main thoroughfare and hailed a taxi. It was another silver Mercedes. As we got in the backseat, he gave the address to the cabbie.

"So you're feeling better, then?" he said.

"I am, thanks."

"Can I make you feel even better?" he asked, tracing my cheek.

"Why not?" I didn't have anything to lose. He seemed like a nice enough guy, and if he'd planned to use force, he would've done it by now.

Owen dipped a finger into the waistband of my pants. The street lamps sparkled, illuminating his face for a second as we passed, then throwing him back into shadow. His fingers moved lower, expertly caressing me like a sable-hair paintbrush on canvas. By the time he was exploring my soft folds, I was almost uncomfortably wet.

"How do you spell your name?" he whispered. "The conventional way?"

The question threw me. "Yeah. One *n* and two *s*'s."

He started by tracing the *V* inside of me. He continued tracing the *a*, *n*, and *e*. My God, I'd spell my name any way he wanted. The buildup was so delicious. When he got to the *s*'s, my hips rocked forward to meet his hand. The *a*—oh, the *a*—was an explosion of light in the dim backseat.

I'd sunk down near the footwell. Owen smiled down at me and lifted me up by the waist.

"That," I said, "was, um, very pleasant."

But now I didn't know what I was supposed to do. Reciprocate? I didn't know how. I started to unzip his jeans.

"No, love," he said. "We're almost there. It's worth the wait, I promise."

Owen paid for the cab, like a gentleman, and pointed toward a building that looked like all the others. He punched in the door code. Rather than going up the stairs, he grabbed a flashlight and ventured down a spiral staircase. The air grew cooler, and I could hear a single drip of water.

I tracked the flashlight's aura. We had to have gone down a good thirty feet.

"Where are we going?" I asked.

"Can't ruin the surprise, love."

The stairs ended. I followed him through a tunnel maybe wide enough for two people abreast. Then I saw the single water drip from the limestone ceiling. A drop landed on my head.

Owen suddenly turned off the flashlight, leaving us in pitch-blackness. He took my hand, and I could hear him patting the wall to find something, and it echoed. Were we in a cave? I remembered that he'd called himself a spelunker.

Owen flipped a switch to reveal a wooden carousel. At the top, round lights lined the scalloped canopy. Horses of all colors, outfitted in elaborate tack, eyes wide. Tinny accordion music played from hidden speakers. It was the most beautiful thing I'd seen in my young life.

"You like it?" Owen asked.

I nodded.

He took my chin in one hand and pressed his lips to mine. My first kiss. It was somehow wetter than I'd expected.

He began to kiss me more firmly, then licked my upper lip. His tongue reached inside my cheek and massaged my tongue in a way that felt instinctive. I found myself leaning into him, wanting to drink from this fountain.

Owen pulled back but held my face in his hands, drawing his thumbs under my eyes and down my cheekbones. I exhaled, louder than I'd meant to. He inserted the tips of his thumbs between my lips.

"I won't bite," Owen said. "Unless you want me to."

I nodded again, afraid that if I said anything, he'd move his hands. No one had ever touched my face with such intimacy. The tips of his thumbs traced my bottom front teeth, then along the ridge of my incisors. I felt the moisture of saliva at the corners of my mouth. I wanted to feel his fingers everywhere. He kissed my forehead and pulled away. I whimpered.

"Let's have a ride, shall we?" Owen said.

As I was choosing a horse, I could see into the next room—another cave, really, with a white screen, projector, and several sofas.

"A theater?" I asked.

"For the underground film scene," Owen said, laughing.

I liked a good pun. Rather than choose the coal-black steed with gray saddle and tassels, the darkness I normally would've preferred, I mounted the white horse with pale-blue accoutrements.

"Ready?" Owen said, his hand on the switch.

"Yes." As the carousel began to turn, I flung my arms outward, embracing everything, even what I couldn't see.

I dreamed of Vince. I was making him macaroni and cheese, our usual fare. The generic kind in a box, or sometimes Kraft. When our mom worked overtime and got a bonus, we got to make fancy macaroni, with mozzarella and Muenster and other real cheeses.

We were playing chess, my favorite. The running joke was that Vince let me win—I lost most of our other games, being the clumsy little sister that I was, but in truth, I'd surpassed him in chess from the day we'd learned the game. It was the only time I had to be merciful, on occasion, and let him win.

We were at a stalemate when I woke up, shivering, in darkness, the only light a soft glow from a nearly melted candle. I could see Owen sleeping on the sofa kitty-corner to mine.

"Oh my God," I said, my words echoing in the cave.

Owen sat straight up. "What is it? What's wrong?"

I didn't think his eyes were even open yet. I was in a cave, under central Paris. Last night I'd taken shrooms and had my first kiss and my first orgasm, though not in that order.

"Owen," I said. "Did we, um . . . ?"

"No, love," he replied. "I prefer my partners to be, shall we say, conscious. You passed out."

"Oh, good. I mean, I'm sure you're lovely—"

"No need to explain. Shall I walk you home?"

"I have no idea where we are. So yes, if you could guide me upstairs and point me toward the Île de la Cité, I'd appreciate it."

He swung his legs forward. "Right, then."

I sat up, too, making sure I had all of my clothing (check) as well as my messenger bag (check). Given the evening's revelry, I was thankful and relieved that I still had my bag.

Owen retrieved the flashlight and blew out the candle. We walked through the tunnel and up the spiral staircase. Today was the day: my trip to the tower. I'd planned this for so many months, but I didn't feel the buoyancy I'd expected.

Once we reached the street, I knew it was still early morning. There were very few people out, just one elderly woman in a kerchief with her shih tzu.

"The metro might be running," said Owen. "Not sure about Sundays."

"I think I'd rather walk," I told him. "Just get me on a relatively easy route to Cité?"

"That I can do."

Entire blocks smelled of fresh bread, a heady, yeasty treat. The next block, however, held the scent of trash, as the garbagemen had yet to pick up the refuse on the sidewalks.

"How long have you lived with Anton and Luc?" I asked.

"Never?" Owen appeared confused. "I live closer to the university."

"So who's their roommate? That Biel guy?"

"No, it's just the two of them in that Belleville flat."

"But they picked us up from the airport," I said. "The taxis were on strike, and they said their roommate's flight was cancelled. They gave us a ride."

"Oh, those cheeky bastards," said Owen. "Was it a white van?"

I nodded.

"They picked up building supplies for the landlord and convinced him to keep the van for a day. They're always talking about American girls. We were having a laugh, and I said they should go to de Gaulle since the taxis were on strike and find some gullible Yankee lasses."

I must've looked at him in horror, because he began to backtrack.

"I didn't think they'd really do it."

I felt nauseated. I'd thought Owen was one of the good guys. "It's fine. No harm, no foul. We're on the Right Bank, yes? Point me toward the river."

"As you wish." He combed his ginger hair back with his fingers. "Keep walking four blocks. Then go right. Walk another couple of kilometers, and you'll be at the Pont Neuf."

"Okay. That's easy enough."

"This is it, then?"

"Owen," I said, "thank you. For everything."

"You're very welcome, love," he said.

I watched him turn around. And when he didn't look back, I started walking. So this was what it was like to share intimacies with another person, to live in the moment, to have no regrets.

I kept walking. Every block, it seemed, had a *boulangerie*. The bakers were hard at work perfecting baguettes for discerning customers. If I'd had any appetite, I could've gone inside to get a fresh one.

Then I realized that I could surprise my friends with a piping hot loaf for breakfast. My friends? My friends! It was the first time, at least that I could remember, calling Whitney and Kiran *mes amies*—even in my head. I recalled there was a *boulangerie* closer to our rental. I wanted it to be as fresh as possible.

Finally, I could see the bridge up ahead. I saw a few more souls out and about. The used booksellers along the quay were drinking coffee and ribbing each other while opening their green wooden lockers filled with first editions, old hardcovers, and racks of post-cards—to appease the tourists, I assumed.

As I crossed the bridge, I could hear the chirping of birds. It grew louder, and some of the disjointed notes morphed into trills and song. I remembered what Anton had said about the flower market: on Sundays, the blossoms had wings.

When I reached the market, I saw the vendors setting out cages. I knew that I had to buy a bird and set it free, just as I'd been allowed my freedom to be (and not to be). Only one other potential customer roamed the central aisle, an old man in a brown suit and fedora. While I was in awe of the vivid colors of the golden parakeets and vermillion parrots and blue macaws, I was drawn to the cage holding simple, common, normally invisible birds: pigeons.

The old man sidled up to me: *"Délicieux."*

His comment, presumably about cooked pigeon, gave me even more incentive to buy one for release.

I asked the vendor, "How much?"

The price he quoted was reasonable, and I had some cash to get rid of anyway. I wanted the one in the corner, the shrinking violet who didn't think she had any worthy songs.

In one quick motion, the vendor covered the bird's eyes and scooped her into a paper sack. I handed over the cash in exchange for the sack.

As I walked to the square in front of Notre-Dame, she rustled.

"Just a few minutes, love," I said. "Then you'll be free."

There was no one in the square, save a city maintenance man, hosing down the area directly in front of the cathedral. I stood in front of Point Zéro, held the bag above my head, and opened it. I saw and heard wings flap above me.

I didn't know if she'd survive long in the wild, but I could imagine her fate if I'd left her in the market. And now she was free.

Because I didn't have a key, I had to ring the doorbell to our rental. I'd bought a baguette for my fellow *Sœurs Rouges*, and it was so fresh from the baker's oven that steam was rising from the top.

Now that I was sober, I had to face the difficult reality of Owen's counsel. I tried convincing myself that I would go through with it, that I'd jump. It was just cold feet, and my Darwinian instinct was attempting to keep me, an individual of the species, alive. An orgasm and a crazy trip on shrooms wouldn't change my life—I'd still end it.

Today, I was certain, everything would change.

Kiran greeted me at the door: "Morning, sunshine. You feel okay?"

"I'm good," I said, and for the first time in a long while, I meant it. "I wasn't too crazy last night, was I?"

"Nah," Kiran said as we walked up the stairs. "But you thought Biel was a doctor who could treat our condition."

"Condition?"

"You thought our eyes were popping out of our heads." Kiran wasn't laughing. She looked tired and defeated by a formidable opponent.

"I'm sorry," I said. "Really."

We entered the kitchen, where Whitney was drinking coffee. She took small sips and held the mug at the level of her face.

"I brought my sisters a fresh baguette!" I waved it in the air before setting it on the counter.

Whitney looked down at her mug. Kiran muttered thanks.

"So did you do the deed with Anton?" I asked. "How was it? Did the lube help?"

"He wasn't—he wasn't worth it," Kiran replied.

I found a bread knife in the drawer and started cutting. The baguette cracked open with the slightest touch of the blade. Then I retrieved the butter and jam from the fridge.

"Bon appétit." I took a hunk of bread for myself.

Neither of them made a move. I felt a little sad, having gone out of my way to bring them breakfast. I thought they liked me.

"Jeez, you guys," I said. "Who died?"

When they didn't respond immediately, I thought I'd lost my chance. I imagined that Kat had been killed in a freak accident, mowed down by a car in the street, or had choked on some tuna at the party, and all of my plans were for naught. That was my first thought—my God, was I a horrible person?

I finally noticed that the double bed in the kitchen alcove where Kat and I had been sleeping was neatly made. Which meant that Kiran or Whitney had slept there, because Kat was the type of person who had others make her bed.

"Where's Kat?" I asked.

Whitney motioned to the closed door. "She wanted the living room to herself. She gave us the bed."

"Um, why?" I asked, drawing out the last word, the long "i" sound.

"She drank a lot last night," Kiran replied. "We carried her home."

Whitney was twirling the short strands of her bangs. "I think she puked most of it up. I'm a little nauseous, too."

"Gross." I liked the drunken buzz, but to be stumbling and vomiting was much less appealing.

"And how are *you* feeling?" Whitney asked.

"Fine." I smiled. "No, better than fine. Good." I knew that many people, once they had a suicide plan, felt relief and then euphoria. Maybe this was my euphoria.

Whitney set her coffee mug on the counter and folded her arms: "Come on. Spill. Tell us about your ginger guy."

I laughed, despite myself. Here I was, acting like a normal teenage girl, ready to tell her friends what she'd done with a boy.

"I don't kiss and tell," I said, playing coy. I wanted to know how much *they* wanted to know before confessing.

"We're in *Paris*," said Kiran. "Truth!"

I was enjoying this normalcy. "Let's just say he gave me an explosion of joy."

"High five." Whitney held up her palm, which I slapped with my own. How . . . normal.

"Thanks."

"So he was fun, huh?" said Whitney.

"Very." I could see a pigeon nosing around outside the kitchen window. "If you guys aren't going to eat that baguette, I'm going to give some to that pigeon."

"Be my guest," said Kiran. Something was off about her—I wondered if Anton had acted creepy or tried something weird.

I wanted to think that bird was the same one I'd released earlier that morning. To be honest, most of them looked alike. It was indeed her, I decided, willing it so. I opened the window and broke off small pieces of bread before tossing them in her direction. Her head bobbed back and forth, her iridescent necklace of green and purple feathers glinting in the sun. I'd never noticed their jeweled collars before—in most light, they just appeared gray.

She found the bread quickly and lifted her beak to force it down her gullet. I imagined her flying from rooftop to rooftop, surveying the beautiful neighborhoods of Paris. Then I remembered that pigeon on the metro tracks, eating through the ribs of a rat carcass.

I shut the window to keep out the morning chill.

"We're going to the Eiffel Tower, right?" I asked.

"I thought we agreed on the afternoon," Whitney said. "Let's let Kat sleep for a while."

"We could get her some *pain au chocolat*," Kiran suggested. "Then maybe walk along the Champs-Élysées and see the Arc de Triomphe."

The itinerary sounded reasonable, though I didn't know why we were rewarding Kat's drunkenness with chocolate. Maybe it was a hangover cure I didn't know about. Apparently, our cease-fire with her was still in effect.

The doorbell rang, an insistent buzz. No one in the city— besides Luc and Anton—had our address. I could see Whitney and Kiran doing the same calculus. The buzzing continued at intermittent intervals. It was loud and jarring.

"Is somebody going to get that?" Kat screamed through the living room door. "I'm trying to sleep. Fucking Christ, do I have to do everything?"

Whitney, Kiran, and I went to the lobby. I had no idea who'd be at the door, and my friends didn't have any better theories.

"Maybe it's your one-night stand," said Whitney.

"I didn't give Owen our address," I assured her. "Honestly."

We opened the door to find a little boy punching the button to our apartment. He looked up at us with dark eyes, expressionless like those of a cow, clutching a soiled bib against his chest. His T-shirt and pants were so dirty that I couldn't determine their original color.

"He's wet," Whitney observed aloud.

"I thought I smelled something," I said, disgusted by the odor. The boy's hair was matted and white streaks ran down his face. "Are those tear tracks?"

"Oh my God," Kiran whispered. "What if he's been abused?"

First Kat's living room barricade and now this little punk. I feared the whole day would be a waste.

Kiran said, "I can't remember the verb for 'to find.' We need to ask if we should find his mother."

"We need to ask if we should find him a diaper," I said. "You really think his mother cares? Come on. Let's take him to the police, and they can deal with him."

Kiran squatted down to be on his level, licked her palm, and wiped away the white crust on his face.

"Hey," Whitney said. "I dare you to, like, take him upstairs and clean him up. Teach him some manners."

"I don't need a dare to do the right thing." Kiran gave us a solemn look. Then she took the boy's hand and proceeded up the stairs with him.

This kid was ruining my plans. Then again, I'd waited this long, so what was another few hours? He climbed two flights of stairs before Kiran picked him up and carried him the rest of the way. I winced. The kid was filthy.

When we got up to the apartment, I noticed that half of the baguette was still on the counter and the living room door remained closed. We three crowded into the bathroom. Kiran set the boy in the tub and, as she took off his shirt, asked his name. The first time he said it, the word was too slurred for us to understand. I guessed he might be deaf and mute.

He tried again: *"Lapin."*

I recognized the word from yesterday's menu. "Is he saying 'rabbit'?"

Kiran held her breath and peeled off the kid's pants. Whitney kept her distance but started the tap, using only the warm faucet.

Just when I didn't think it was possible for the kid to smell worse, I caught another whiff. He assaulted my senses in so many ways: visual, olfactory, and now auditory, as he started to whine. Kiran had just squirted shampoo all over his body and left for a moment to put his dirty clothes in the tiny washing machine under the kitchen counter.

Then he began flicking his penis.

"Oh *hell* no," Whitney said, slapping his hand away. "Bad."

This sequence of flicking and slapping played out several more times, until Whitney whacked him across the face and made him whimper.

Kiran had returned. "Jeez, you can't do that, Whit. Don't you think that's how he got that way in the first place?"

"I'm just, like, trying to teach him some decency," Whitney replied. "Never too early to stop a guy from thinking with his dick, right?"

I thought it was funny, but no one laughed. Her red handprint remained on his cheek.

Kiran turned on the overhead shower full blast to rinse the little boy. He closed his eyes and then spit water on her. She wiped it from her cheek and soldiered on.

The boy spoke: *"Glacée. Je veux la crème glacée."*

He wanted ice cream.

"Glacée," he insisted.

Kiran wrapped him in a cocoon of clean towels. As I studied his small body and wizened older face, I felt a pang of tenderness for the boy.

"He can wear one of my T-shirts," said Kiran. "Can you guys contribute underwear or something?"

"Unless he wants to wear a thong, um, no," replied Whitney.

I had a pair of gray Hanes undies that I donated to the cause.

Kiran gently lifted the towels from his body and pulled a navy Washington High Swim Team T-shirt over his head. She also slid my gray Hanes up and over his pelvis. The undies were a little baggy, but the ridiculous T-shirt hung to his knees.

Kiran tried hugging him, but he started flicking her cheek.

"Shouldn't we take him to the police?" I asked. "I mean, we're not social workers."

"Wait a minute," said Kiran. "I can't just ignore it when bad things happen. Can we just get him some ice cream and take him to the park? We do something nice for the poor kid. Then the police. Okay?"

Whitney and I acquiesced. Kat wasn't up yet anyway, so it wasn't as though we'd be going to *la tour Eiffel* in the next couple of hours.

The three of us, plus the little rabbit boy, sat in wicker chairs outside a touristy café by Notre-Dame. His silky hair had dried, and since it fell past his ears, he resembled a young girl. His pants had still been wet when we left the apartment, so we cinched the Wash High Swim Team T-shirt with a belt, further contributing to his girlish look.

Lapin had chosen chocolate ice cream. He was either unaccustomed to using utensils or just messy. Kiran had bought him a cup rather than a cone to try and circumvent this issue, but he refused to use the spoon. Instead, he plunged his face directly into the cup. The ice cream dripped down his chin and onto his shirt, where it looked like mud.

"He's freaking hopeless," said Whitney.

"Maybe that's his con," I said. "He lures tourists to buy him ice cream. All of his dirt is really just chocolate."

"I don't think so." Kiran lowered her voice to a whisper. "He's like autistic or mentally challenged."

A couple next to us, tall and Nordic looking, kept stealing glances at us. They were drinking coffee and eating crêpes laden with strawberries.

"Ness, you have the guidebook with you?" Kiran asked.

"Yep."

"Can you look up kid-friendly stuff to do?"

"Sure." I remembered that such a section existed in the guidebook, but I'd had no reason to pay attention to it. I had to look it up in the index. It was on page ninety-one and labeled "Child's Play" in a goofy font.

The Nordic woman politely asked if one of us would take their picture. So that was why they'd been staring. Whitney volunteered, and they thanked her profusely.

"We've taken hardly any photos," Whitney said. "I brought like ten rolls of film, and I want to use them."

"Go ahead." I put an arm around Lapin's shoulder. "Cheese!"

He pushed me away with both hands before returning to the ice cream, which he'd almost finished.

"Eeyore," she said. "That's borderline. That's like attempted puppy murder."

"Huh?" said Kiran.

"Every time Nessa's a downer, a puppy dies," explained Whitney.

"Disneyland Paris." I was reading from the Child's Play section. "Sounds pricey. How about the Jardin du Luxembourg? There's a puppet theater and sailboat pond and pony rides."

"But seriously," said Whitney. "We don't have any pictures of us together. Like, the Red Sisters."

"Shouldn't we include Kat?" asked Kiran, shifting in her wicker chair. "She took a bullet for us last night."

"Is someone going to tell me what happened?" I said.

Whitney and Kiran exchanged looks.

"I don't normally drink very much," Kiran said, her eyes filling with tears. "I—I—"

"No, let me tell it," Whitney interrupted. "Kiran, it wasn't your fault. Anton kept talking about the Negro princess thing. So Kat did what she does best—she got to be the center of attention."

I vaguely remembered seeing the closed bedroom door and hearing squeaking bedsprings. Despite all of Kat's big talk, she was probably hungover *and* ashamed that she'd stolen Anton from Kiran.

"Okay, say no more. I get it." I stood up from the table. "Luxembourg Gardens?"

According to the map, the park was within walking distance. Lapin, for his part, gripped Kiran's hand and was well behaved until we arrived at the gardens. He ran, full speed, toward a lady with a rainbow bouquet of balloons.

"Lapin!" Kiran shouted.

The lady was quick—she extended her arm to the sky, putting the balloons out of reach.

"Quelle couleur?" Kiran asked him.

"Orange!"

She handed the lady a five-franc note. Just ahead, I spotted the puppet theater and a crowd of small children with their caretakers buying tickets.

"Lapin," I said. "Look! Marionettes!"

He seemed much more interested in the balloon bobbing from his wrist. Which turned out to be fine, given that the theater charged admission and the next show wasn't for another hour. The poster depicted old-fashioned puppets, probably papier-mâché, with ruddy blisters for cheeks. I found them charming, even though one was clubbing the other.

A few kids around us chattered with excitement. Lapin just stared at them, blank eyed. Then he looked back to his orange balloon.

"Pipi," he said. Just as quickly as it began, he started repeating the word, screaming, *"Pipi!"*

Whitney was the first to find the public restrooms. For a few moments, we wrestled with whether to send him into the men's restroom or accompany him into the women's. But he refused to move and wouldn't go into either restroom. I couldn't blame the kid—a park bathroom was sure to be disgusting. He continued to scream and was starting to garner attention from the other kids as well as the adults.

Kiran squatted down to his level and tried to hug him. Then he began slapping his cheek, really hitting himself hard. That, combined with the screaming, produced a kind of TV-Indian war cry. The scene was so absurd I had to hold back laughter.

"We're taking him to the police now," hissed Whitney.

We heard the shrill blast of a whistle because we'd attracted the attention of a gendarme. I was relieved—I didn't know how we'd manage to get the kid, who was now literally kicking and screaming, to the police station.

Kiran and I struggled to communicate with the gendarme because neither of us could remember the French word for "lost." In the end, we just used English.

"Of course," he said. "I will remedy, of course."

Lapin seemed comforted by the authority figure. He stopped the war cry and even bid us adieu.

I keep a shoebox of mementos from the trip. I take it out maybe once a year, and I'm always careful to wrap it in holiday-themed paper so if anyone found it, it'd look like a Christmas present. Both Cricket and my husband love surprises, so even if one of them discovered it, they wouldn't want to spoil the surprise.

I carefully unwrap the snowflake-print paper from the box, which once housed a pair of sensible work pumps—I'd gone up a size after pregnancy. I take off the lid and make a mental inventory of its contents. Everything is accounted for: the blank Père Lachaise postcard, metro stubs from the Cité stop, a feather from the pigeon I'd bought, those cheesy affirmation notecards, and the blonde tassel of hair. That's what always gets me, the hair, which I'd bound together with a red ribbon, in honor of *les Sœurs Rouges*. Undamaged by chemical dyes, it remains silky and smooth. I hold it up to my face. Year after year, it always smells the same—faintly of ripe strawberries, the last bit of sweetness before the fruit begins to rot.

Whitney, Kiran, and I made our way back to the apartment. As it was Sunday, late morning, the streets began to fill with Parisians and tourists alike. To have full use of his hand for slapping, Lapin had given his orange balloon to Kiran, who still had it looped round her wrist.

"So," Whitney said, as we were approaching the bridge to Île de la Cité. "File that under embarrassing."

"I couldn't just stand there and do nothing," Kiran said. "Not again."

"God Kiran, let it go," insisted Whitney. "You're not guilty of anything."

"A monkey stole my camera when I was in India. And bit me," said Kiran.

Whitney laughed, indicating this was an acceptable moment, so I laughed, too. In the scheme of things, it *was* funny, hilarious even, that we'd taken in a street urchin and thought we could help him. Kiran seemed to think that a bath and a trip to the park would solve everything.

"Could've been worse," I said. "He could've told the police that we kidnapped him."

"Eeyore," said Whitney, "that's, like, glass-half-full kind of talk."

"I'm still a half-empty pessimist, don't worry."

"Whatever," Kiran said. "Look for a *boulangerie* so we can get Kat a *pain au chocolat*."

Kiran held up her fist and the balloon, letting the orange orb float up to the heavens.

We did find a *boulangerie*—they were ubiquitous—and Kiran got a *pain au chocolat* for Kat. She held the warm pastry in wax paper as we trudged up the apartment stairs. I couldn't help but feel that I'd missed something essential—I had a hard time understanding why we were bringing Kat breakfast in bed. She'd stolen Anton, and now Kiran was groveling? Was this some kind of girl friendship thing I didn't understand?

Kiran knocked on the living room door. "Kat? How're you doing?"

"Shitty," yelled Kat, who refused to open the door. "I'm in a world of hurt."

"We got you some *pain au chocolat*."

"I don't want that shit," Kat yelled. "I want something familiar. Get me deep-dish pizza like Giordano's. Pepperoni and sausage."

"You heard her," said Kiran. "Nessa, can you check the guidebook? Any Chicago-style pizza close by?"

I looked, but only out of loyalty to Kiran—certainly not to Kat. I remembered a handful of pizza places, but none of them deep-dish. I was pretty sure that the style was unique to the States.

I pored over the guidebook and finally found a restaurant called Angelo's, over on the Right Bank. I read aloud: "A festive place with limited seating and serviceable deep-dish pizza. As of this writing, the only Chicago-style pies in the city."

"Let's go," ordered Kiran.

It was clear that Kat wasn't going to the Eiffel Tower without having pizza first. I just hoped the pizza would lure her out of bed. The morning after a party, Vince had always wanted a big, greasy breakfast: fried eggs with cheese, hash browns with butter, and lots of bacon. Kat was obviously craving greasy food for her hangover.

So we three made our way downstairs and headed for the Right Bank.

"I don't get why she's being so difficult," I said. "I'm sure hangovers suck, but she's being melodramatic."

The bird market was in full swing. Kiran and Whitney marveled at the exotic caged birds. Besides buying winged pets (or, presumably, dinner), people could purchase birdseed and antique cages. A few parents brought their kids to see the parrots and canaries.

As we continued, I recognized the path I'd taken earlier that morning, on my way back from Owen's place. Actually, I didn't even know where he lived, and had only a vague recollection of the apartment building over those underground caves we'd explored. It hadn't looked distinct from any of the other buildings.

I shivered with the memory of that magical carousel. Had I really just described something as magical? I didn't believe in magic. I believed in cold, hard reality.

And of course, in reality, Angelo's was closed on Sundays.

"We've failed," said Kiran, and I thought I saw her eyes water. The sun was bright, and she wasn't wearing sunglasses.

"We'll find something else," Whitney said. "A gift maybe?"

"What, like soap?" Kiran said, her voice choking into a sob. "Like Summer's Eve douche? Do you think they make a Hallmark card that says 'Sorry you got gangbanged'?"

"Slow down," I said, hurt they'd hidden the truth from me, and not altogether believing that Kat's bed-springing escapades could possibly be forced. "Will someone tell me *exactly* what happened last night?"

"The vodka did me in," said Kiran, tears running down her cheeks. "I let Anton—I mean—"

Had Kiran been assaulted? I felt my own eyes tear up.

"Let me tell it," said Whitney, sighing. "Anton pulled Kiran into his room. Kat and I stood outside the door—the Negro princess thing was creepy, so we just wanted to make sure everything was okay. Then Luc came up and shoves his hand up my skirt and goes, 'The prophet likes his disciple, yes?' and laughs. Then, before Kat and I can even react, Luc goes in. So we follow him in."

"And then?" I asked. I didn't understand. How could anyone hurt Kiran? She was the best among us.

Whitney continued: "Kat goes, 'Come on, boys, she's got zero skills. Doesn't even know what she's doing. But I do—even says so on my back.' Then she takes her shirt off and they're both groping her and she makes me and Kiran leave the bedroom. Kat was, like, possessed and just kept saying 'Get the fuck out of here!' in this weird whisper-scream."

I was so relieved that Kiran was okay. But I'd forgotten about the sign we'd made Kat wear. "But wasn't it like a crazy ménage à trois? I heard the bedsprings and them going at it when I left."

"I was drunk and stupid," Kiran said. "I was so relieved. We went back to the balcony, and Biel gave us another wine and Coke."

"Kiran, I'm telling you," Whitney said, crying and grabbing Kiran's shoulders, "it wasn't your fault."

Their behavior started to make sense. They'd been speaking in code, not wanting to admit to themselves, or each other, their culpability in this mess. It also explained why Kiran had been hell-bent about helping the little boy and not being a bystander.

That was when it dawned on me: despite Whitney's initial version of the story, Kat hadn't willingly slept with Anton and Luc. She'd sacrificed herself so Kiran (and even Whitney) didn't get hurt. Maybe Kat had been raped. And maybe she wasn't as evil as I'd thought.

Seeing Kiran and Whitney's anguish, their twisted red faces, I felt the familiar sting in my eyes. Their expressions confirmed my hunch. Somehow Kat knew that Luc and Anton were predators, determined to have their way with a dumb American girl. I remembered Owen telling me about their airport quest—there was no roommate to pick up. We were the only girls at the party, which I didn't fully recognize at the time. And when I remembered that stupid question I'd asked Kat about her preference, rape or murder ("Kill me. No question."), I wept openly.

Ah, yes, the best-laid plans o' mice and men. But what of young girls?

The three of us returned to the apartment with the French version of the Quarter Pounder, a "Royal Cheese" (almost, but not quite, a Royale with Cheese) along with a large fry and a vanilla milkshake. We were surprised that McDonald's served beer, and we split one just for the novelty. It was bitter and disgusting and reminded me why I'd spit out my sip of Vince's Natty Light.

Kiran knocked on the living room door. "Hey, Kat. The only place in the city with deep-dish is closed on Sundays. So we got you a Royale with Cheese. I hope that's okay."

To our surprise, she opened the door. She was wearing a blanket over her head like a hooded cape and accepted the paper bag of food.

"Do you want us to run a bath for you or anything?" Whitney asked.

"Nah. I'd rather shower later," she said. "Thanks. You can come in if you want."

We all sat down on the striped cushions while Kat started on the burger. The blanket fell around her shoulders.

"Not bad," she said.

How could I possibly make my fatal leap in front of Kat? The worst thing she could imagine had happened the night before. She'd gotten more than enough punishment for one lifetime. The solution was to leap without any of the girls seeing me.

"Didn't you guys get anything to eat?" Kat asked, her mouth full of burger.

"No," Kiran replied. "It seemed, well, disrespectful."

"Ah. Just because I got gangbanged last night doesn't mean I'm not the same bitch I was before." Kat dipped fries, two at a time, in ketchup.

"We did split a beer," said Whitney, sheepishly. "We couldn't believe they, like, sell beer at McDonald's."

"Do you want to go to the police?" I asked.

Kat set down the burger, and I knew that I'd said the wrong thing. "It's their word against mine. I can't even speak the language. And any witnesses at the party? Remember that I was literally wearing a sign that said 'SLUT.' So no. End of discussion."

"I'm really sorry," I said, and meant every word.

"It was an honest question," Kat said. "From now on, no more kid gloves. It's just a normal day in Europe, and we're going to do normal tourist things. Like see the Eiffel Tower."

My stomach lurched in my throat. I'd wanted this for so long that I'd conditioned myself to be excited. But the recent sequence of events had me questioning everything. I knew that I wouldn't jump in front of Kat—she had her own demons to battle now. But did I want to leap at all? I hadn't planned for anything after Paris. I had nothing.

Kat polished off all the food, sucking down the last of the milkshake.

"You want to hear something funny?" Whitney asked.

"Always."

"I slapped a little kid who was playing with his penis," Whitney said. "I figured it's never too early to stop a guy from thinking with his dick, right?"

"She slapped him hard," Kiran added.

"No shit." Kat giggled. "*That* is spectacular. Okay, I just need a shower, and then we'll go."

Kiran, Whitney, and I remained on the cushions. I didn't know what to do—I hoped I'd figure it out when I was high above the city, at the top of the tower. Such a view might provide insight.

We all sat there in silence. What was there to say?

Cricket has never questioned her paternity, despite Daniel's sandy blond hair, now thinning at the temples, and his pale skin that burns within minutes of being in the sun. But she's never had any reason to.

Her hair is just a shade or two lighter than black, much thicker and wavier than mine, but her skin is olive. Her swim team practices outdoors in the summers, and she turns golden brown. She's surprisingly athletic (especially given my physical awkwardness) and may even get a scholarship to swim in college—she's that good.

After practice, she sits at the kitchen island, pivoting the bar stool left and right as she works on French vocab.

"Mom," she says, in between bites of orange wedges, "did you know that *pari* means 'bet' or 'risk'? The plural, *paris*, means risks."

I did not, I tell her. But how appropriate.

Cricket separates the last bite of orange from the peel and puts the peel over her teeth like a mouth guard. She smiles, revealing a ridiculous bright-orange cartoon grin.

That girl has me wrapped around her little finger.

From the metro station, we followed the mass of tourists a few blocks to the Eiffel Tower. Under the arches, North African immigrants hawked Eiffel key chains, one franc each. Dark netting and scaffolding covered part of the monument that was being restored or painted. To protect the iron, I knew that it had to be repainted every seven years, which took sixty tons of paint.

Tour groups got to enter through a separate gate. The guides held little flags or umbrellas in the air to signal their packs of eager tourists. Somehow we were in the middle of three different groups—Japanese, German, and Italian—with each of the guides giving what I assumed to be introductions and Eiffel history. I wanted to tell them what Owen had revealed to me, that one of Eiffel's engineers had actually designed *la Dame de Fer*. Maurice Koechlin. But he was forgotten, a casualty of Eiffel's ego.

I didn't understand why the French called it the Iron Lady. Yes, its base could be construed as a lattice skirt, but everything else was hard and angular. Its tip pierced the sky. It dominated the view of the city. Surely it was male rather than female?

The other girls were debating whether to take ground photos before or after we went up. I lobbied for after, since I didn't want to waste any more time. The ticket clerks and security guards looked infinitely bored.

As our purses were being searched, I wondered what a bomb even looked like. Wouldn't it be disguised as something else? I felt ready to explode. I didn't know whether I'd die that day or be reborn. Both seemed equally likely.

We were inside the bottom of the tower now, which had antiquated gears and elevators, everything mechanical like the guts of an old clock. There were gawking people everywhere, which was ruining my experience. I wanted time alone with my obsession. And I wanted transcendence, to feel a sense of the sacred—I was finally here. But the place just felt like a tourist trap.

"Check it out," Kat said, flicking her Zippo to reveal a flame. "Security didn't take this."

"They wouldn't want to deny anyone their God-given right to smoke," Kiran said.

"I wonder how long it takes for skin to burn," said Kat. "If there's a lot of fat underneath, wouldn't it be faster?"

She held the flame toward me.

I didn't flinch. I wasn't afraid. In fact, I was starting to feel sorry for her. Her punishment from Anton and Luc didn't fit her crime. What happened after you experience the worst thing you can imagine?

We were herded onto the next open elevator, the only nod to modern technology being a digital scale. The operator appeared as though he should've been enjoying retirement rather than ferrying people up and down a giant phallus. He watched the red numbers flicker until the elevator reached capacity in metric tons, and he had to turn the last person away. The doors closed. My stomach lurched, jumping in my throat, as if I were on an amusement ride.

I remembered that the monument was always meant to be temporary, to be torn down around 1910. Eiffel had set up a meteorological lab and invited scientists to do the same in order to secure his legacy. I'd read that during World War II, the French shut down the elevators so the invading Germans wouldn't get to see the spectacular views of the city. Hitler was too lazy to take the stairs, and he ordered the tower to be dismantled. While the acting general disobeyed, someone managed to fly the Nazi flag at the very top.

Through the elevator glass, I could see the stairs, but I didn't see anyone using them. The first platform of the tower had two restaurants and a seasonal garden. And the view wasn't bad—all those gray buildings of Paris, the Seine bisecting them like a thick tapeworm. But everything seemed so small, insignificant. Wind rustled my hair. The wind also kept extinguishing the flame of Kat's lighter as she tried to run it along the skin of her forearm.

"Do I need to take that away from you?" asked Kiran.

"You little pyro!" said Whitney, but the joke fell flat.

"Come on, let's go see the top!" I said, trying to sound more excited than nervous.

I needed a sign to know what to do. I was surprised to notice that, up close, it became clear the iron was painted brown, the color of a paper bag. What did that mean? Appearances were deceiving? What did that have to do with anything?

We found the line to go up to the next floor. It was even longer than the previous one. A middle-aged British couple reached the line just before us, and the woman groaned.

"Ah, well," she said. She wore a tracksuit with gold zippers and a gold-sequined purse to match. "It'll be worth it, right? Have to do it once in your life."

The line inched forward. Because the queue weaved around dividers to save space, we were always seeing the same people. Like the two matching Japanese couples, the young women huddling into their boyfriends to stay out of the wind. Or the trio of slick Mediterranean guys who must have had to buy economy-sized tubes of hair gel. And, of course, the British couple:

"We left Dad at the gift shop with Jess. What if she loses 'im?"

Her similarly tracksuited husband told her not to worry: "He'll show up."

For whatever reason, I hadn't given any thought to the other people who'd be at the tower, and I was irritated to spend time with them, hearing about their trivial problems.

"Okay," I said. "Let's play Truth. Have either of you ever thought about suicide?"

"Yeah," Whitney admitted. "But not seriously. For a few minutes maybe."

"Who hasn't?" said Kat. "Everybody feels hopeless once in a while."

There's a difference, I thought, *between feeling hopeless and actually having no hope, no future.*

"Kiran?" I asked. "What about you?"

"No."

"Come on," Kat said. "Not even once? When you were overwhelmed gunning for valedictorian and president of everything, you never glanced at a bottle of Tylenol and wondered how many you could take and just fall asleep?"

"Be honest." I was so frustrated by her relentless optimism. "I mean it. When life is difficult, there's always another option. It's a failure of imagination *not* to think about it."

"I honestly haven't. Jeez," she said. "What do you think happens when you die, anyway?"

"I don't know," I replied truthfully. "Maybe it's like before you were born. Just, nothing." But I wanted to believe that I'd see Vince. Wasn't that what I believed? Why was I doubting myself now?

"Well, I think there's a heaven," said Whitney.

"Maybe," Kat said. "There's definitely a hell."

"My family believes in reincarnation," said Kiran. "But I don't know."

"So if you're good, you'll be reincarnated as a rich supermodel?" Whitney said, laughing. I was amused by her ideal.

"It's a little more complicated than that."

We'd reached the front of the line for the second elevator. The attendant barked at us to move to the back, in both French and English. When he pressed the button to take everyone up, I noticed he had only half a pinky finger.

Finally, we'd arrived—we were on top of the world. I pushed off the elevator first, the others close behind, all finding the view obstructed by a steel cage. I'd hoped for insight, but all I felt was emptiness.

"I thought we'd be able to see better," Whitney said, shouting over the wind.

"You can," said Kiran, "if you get really close." She pushed her nose through one of the diamond-shaped openings.

The city spread before us. Below the cloudy sky, the buildings seemed more pale lavender, like a fading bruise, than gray. The river snaked through the old architecture. From here, the river tore through the city like a knife through a priceless, if drab, masterpiece. I stared at the river a while longer, and near one of the islands, saw a small replica of the Statue of Liberty. On the other side, traffic buzzed along the busy thoroughfare, the cars zipping like pixels of a video game.

While Whitney and Kiran snapped photos, I went up a couple of steps into a glass-enclosed vestibule filled with people escaping the gale-force wind. The informational placards above the windows showed flags of the world and distances from various cities. With all the people crowded inside, the view wasn't any better.

I stepped back outside, the wind whipping my hair into my face. I kept exploring the perimeter, trying to stay out of people's photos, and found a viewing panel into Eiffel's secret apartment. Wax figures of Gustave and his daughter showed them entertaining Thomas Edison. Dark paisley wallpaper and a burgundy Oriental rug outfitted the small apartment. Despite the two men's hand gestures, which indicated a passionate scientific conversation, their expressions were indifferent.

I did not want indifference. I wanted a sign, something clear. But nothing was obvious to me.

Whitney found me and looped her arm through mine. "Come on! Kat's buying champagne."

She led me to a small counter with an attendant serving chilled bottles.

The price of a bottle was exorbitant, the same as one night of our rental.

"Whoa, it's expensive," Kiran said.

We had to huddle together to hear each other.

Kat whipped out a credit card. "Don't worry. It's on Daddy."

Kat ordered a bottle and we toasted to being "on top." The bubbles tickled the roof of my mouth. I couldn't help but feel like this was a prelude to our good-byes—no matter what happened, I suspected we'd never see each other again. We polished off the bottle in record time, with Kat drinking two and a half glasses.

"I feel better," she said. "And now I'm going to get a better view. One that's not obstructed."

That was supposed to be my line. Once again, Kat was stealing from me. An older Irish couple interrupted us.

"Sorry to bother, dears, but my husband would like a photo with you lovely ladies," said the woman, close enough that I could smell her coffee breath. "Would you oblige him?"

Kiran agreed before any of us could object. The Irish man grinned ear to ear, dentures glistening, his baldness pink and shiny. Kiran and Kat went on one side of him while Whitney and I took the other. He put two wrinkled, age-spotted arms around us. I put my arm around Whitney's shoulder. I smiled, baring my teeth like an animal.

"Say Paris!" the woman yelled before snapping a picture. "Oh, another? One more?"

"Beautiful," the old man clucked in a thick Irish brogue.

"Thank you, girls," said the woman. "You have certainly made his day."

What I wouldn't give for a copy of that photo. After all the media coverage, I'd hoped the couple would come forward with it. I hoped in vain. I wanted something that showed us all smiling.

If Kat wanted an unobstructed view, I'd help her find it. There were too many barriers on the top level of the tower—we'd have to go back down to the second level.

The elevator descended in a hydraulic hiss, and we stepped off.

"What about there?" I asked, pointing to an area that appeared to be under construction. It was less windy on the second platform, but I still had to speak louder than normal.

"Vanessa," Kat said, leaning in, "what would I do without you?"

"I think you'd survive."

We walked over to investigate. It could've been an ideal spot, but it didn't feel right. And I realized that, for all my bravado, I was absolutely terrified. Owen had been right. I'd been so focused on my plan, and then stubbornly trying to prove him wrong, that I wouldn't admit how scared I was. That I might actually want to live. That hope was more difficult to feel than despair.

"You can climb up that one—put your foot in the middle of the X's," Kiran said.

But what would I do? College was out of the question. Maybe I could see more of the world. Learn other languages. Read all of the books I'd been meaning to get to.

I looked up to see Kat trembling. Her face was pale and shiny with sweat. She'd scaled nearly ten feet when I realized her intentions. *No,* I thought, *no.* Yet I could understand her reasons—she couldn't cheat her way through college, her married boyfriend wouldn't exactly miss her, and the night before, she'd experienced the worst thing she could imagine. Her identity as a bold, sexual young woman had been taken from her. And I had reminded her of a solution, with my babble about suicide.

We were one and the same. She couldn't foresee a future for herself and thought there was only one way out.

Kiran, seeing her friend's hesitation, followed. She was athletic and nimble, climbing up the girder, stopping just below Kat.

"Kat," she said. "I'm right here, okay? We all care about you. Now come down."

"But I . . ." Kat said, her voice faint. She didn't finish her sentence.

"Seriously," said Whitney, her neck craned upward. "We all love you, even if we don't always show it."

"I'm not afraid," Kat shouted.

"We know," Kiran said. "You're a badass. But we still need you here with us. So come down."

By that point, a crowd of gawkers had formed around us. I was frozen in place. That was supposed to be me up there. I was supposed to be looking down at the world, pitying all of the suckers dumb enough to have hope. And here I was, holding a flash of hope for myself, like a firefly in a jar. I wanted—no, I needed—for it to grow bigger and illuminate everything.

"Remind me," said Kat. "Who got gang-raped? Was it any of *you*? No? I didn't think so."

"We'll help you heal," said Kiran.

"Unless you have a time machine, you can't help."

"You're wrong," said Kiran. "I'm going to grab your foot and hold it until you get down. And I'm a very patient person. I can wait all day."

I tried to speak some words of encouragement, but nothing came out.

As Kiran grabbed Kat's foot, Kat kicked her hand away. The unexpected kick sent Kiran off balance. Her arms flailed behind her, as if she were doing a slow-motion backstroke. Even as it was happening, my mind failed to connect the details, simply refused to believe.

Her scream. Of all the details, I don't remember the pitch of her scream. I remember it fading as she fell to the ground, but the tone still eludes me. Somehow it feels disrespectful to her memory.

I like to think that her death was merciful, that she had a heart attack midair, that her brain flooded with endorphins. That she didn't feel the impact. That she had no idea her body, upon smashing into the ground, would make a hole six inches deep and two feet wide.

I can't tell you how grateful I am that she perished before the advent of iPhones and other recording devices. I can't stand the thought of her death being on video, available to voyeurs. The only tourist with a camcorder, thankfully, wasn't very quick on the draw—he was able to capture some footage of officials carrying away her broken corpse, but with the gawking crowd, all you could see were her dangling legs.

It's also a small mercy that her falling body didn't hit anyone on the ground. That was something I didn't think about when I'd planned to jump, something that I was too shortsighted to even consider.

Kat, Whitney, and I were escorted inside the police station in the Île de la Cité, in the center of Paris. Were we transported in police cars? I don't know. We must've been, because I do remember the sirens, and how the French ones were distinct from their American counterparts. Here in the States, the sirens are multitonal and go *WEEEEE-ee-yo*, *WEEEEE-ee-yo*, *WEEEEE-ee-yo*, but the French emergency blasts are different. They're only two-tone: *err-RUHR, err-RUHR, err-RUHR . . .*

Or maybe that was the sound of the ambulance that took her body away.

Whitney was strangely stoic, probably from shock. Kat and I wept openly, our faces red and contorted, our vision blinded from tears. I discovered that Kat was not my enemy but my sister. She had only been trying to make the best of a bad situation and used the resources at her disposal, just like I had. When she couldn't see a way out, she decided to leave this world. And her selfishness caused significant collateral damage. I'd been fighting her this whole time only to realize that she was simply too much like me to appreciate.

"I killed her," Kat said between sobs. "I fucking killed her."

"No," I said. "*We* killed her."

"It was an accident," Whitney insisted, dry-eyed, in shock. "Accidents happen."

I cried even more, until I felt parched and void of feeling. I passed out on a hard plastic chair. I woke up drooling and disoriented, only to remember that I'd helped kill a girl I considered my friend.

Each of us was questioned by the French police. To the best of my knowledge, we all told the truth: it was a horrible accident. A series of dares gone wrong. A dear friend who, seeing another in danger, tried to help.

The French authorities were satisfied by our answers. Eyewitness accounts corroborated our stories. Because we were eighteen, and her death was ruled an accident rather than a suicide, her name was released and a media circus ensued. To think—I'd been naïve enough to assume that my leap would be publicized, but it all hinged on intent (or lack thereof, in her case). Journalists found her yearbook photos, her senior portrait, and her sports team pictures. They interviewed her classmates and old teammates. Her beautiful smile graced the pages of major publications. A pretty young girl in her prime, a tragedy at the most iconic monument in the world—it was far too sensational to let rest.

But among the three of us, we didn't give one word to the reporters. No one else could have her. We locked our secrets away and threw the key into the murky Seine. Her family was silent, too. They wished for a private memorial.

For us, the survivors, her death was just too much for our nascent friendship to bear. I knew I'd never see Kat and Whitney again. Whitney's sister took the next flight from O'Hare to de Gaulle, and Kat's mother postponed her dig near Damascus to accompany her daughter home. Kat's parents booked her a stay at a private, residential health clinic in Taos, New Mexico—"a loony-bin-slash-spa," Kat joked, probably the only thing we laughed about on that awful day.

We e-mailed each other several times over the next few months. Whitney still wanted to be a wedding planner and was headed to U of I in the fall. Kat decided to pursue acting in New York—she'd met a director in Taos. Her father was "not happy but coming around" because she promised to try out for Oscar Wilde plays and eventually apply to Yale drama.

I did see Kat one more time, about a year ago, flipping through the channels at 1:00 a.m. I settled on an episode of *Law & Order*. She was less recognizable without her signature black bob, but her laugh was the same. Kat's character stumbled out of a nightclub, and in the next scene, the detectives were examining her body somewhere in Central Park. It was so eerie that I snapped off the television and sat there on the sofa for what could've been minutes or hours, I don't really know.

I didn't take my scheduled flight home from Paris. I was glad I'd traveled light, with only my messenger bag and a few clothes. I didn't need much. And I was glad I'd forgotten to mail that postcard to my mother. I sent her a different one, saying I'd be staying here for a while. I left it vague and open-ended to ensure I had choices.

I wanted revenge on Luc and Anton, but I was having difficulty coming up with a plan. This was where I usually excelled. Since I still had the rental for a week, I wondered if I could lure them into the apartment and drug their wine. But then what would I do? I didn't have it in me to go all-out Lorena Bobbitt. Maybe if I'd been raped, I could have mustered the courage to mutilate them, but the truth was that I hadn't experienced that kind of suffering. And it wasn't as though I had easy access to barbiturates or tranquilizers.

I considered enlisting Owen's help. I thought he might be a sympathetic ear and could probably get me something to drug them with, but then I remembered that he was the one who'd suggested taking the van and finding some naïve American girls at the airport. Even in jest, he'd helped set the events in motion. I desperately wanted to remember him riding the magical underground carousel, not as my accomplice (or worse, friend of Luc and Anton).

What, exactly, was the use? My grand plan of revenge against Kat didn't work out—it had caused more harm than good. Even if I could somehow hurt Luc and Anton, I figured it would all be in vain. John Wayne Bobbitt had raped and abused his wife. Sure, he had his penis cut off, but it was reattached and then he starred in a porno. People all around the world had sympathy for the guy— and he wasn't the true victim. So violence against Luc and Anton seemed futile.

Kat had sacrificed herself. Maybe I could do the same and save another girl, one I'd never know. But maybe it'd be one less girl looking down, peering off the ledge, deciding whether to jump because the pain was so bad. And in doing so, destroying another life, an innocent who was trying to help. I realized that I wanted punishment for my crimes, not retribution for Luc and Anton's.

Once again, I found solace in books. I'd heard from another avid reader that one of Paris's English-language bookstores, Shakespeare and Company, would put up wayward souls in exchange for working at the store. It turned out the accommodations were basic, on the benches and floors of the shop, which didn't bother me—for a second time that year, I cried myself to sleep every night. I gladly alphabetized and stocked, taking the occasional break to delve into a novel. But I didn't have the attention span that I once did. I kept thinking about what I had to do. And gearing up to do it. I needed punishment in order to forgive myself.

One evening, after downing nearly a bottle of red wine, I took the metro to Luc and Anton's place. I waited in the lobby, a little woozy, but by that time, mostly sober. I wanted them to hurt me like they'd hurt Kat, and in turn, Kiran. I was ready to serve my time.

Luc opened the door. I could see Anton sitting in a wicker chair, smoking.

"Come in," Luc said, extending his hand and showing that movie-star smile.

I knew I was headed into the lion's den. Was I ready for them to tear me apart? I took a deep breath and stepped inside.

I'd postponed my return flight yet again and stayed in Paris for another three months or so. For the first time in my life, I had no plan. Although the Eiffel Tower was a bleak reminder, I tried to forget by seeking novel experiences. I told myself I'd done all I could by sacrificing myself to Luc and Anton's sick pleasures, had literally felt the pain that had precipitated everything. That maybe I'd saved some poor girl from being raped—that I'd satisfied their appetite for a while. I divorced myself from the sequence of events by calling it "the tragedy" or "the accident," even in my head.

I read books. I formed intense friendships with other travelers at the bookstore, the kind of intimacy that can only be achieved when you spend a few days with someone and know you'll never see them again. Some of the savvy regulars taught me the tricks of the trade—where to get free meals without resorting to the Hare Krishnas, exactly when the bibliophile gym attendant worked because she let us in to take showers. One of the old bakers in the *boulangerie* down the block was convinced that I looked exactly like his first love, so he gave me a fresh baguette every day.

It was the baker who first called me *rondelette*, or chubby. He joked that he was giving me too much bread. And I realized that I was eating for two.

I hadn't been worried about missing my period for several months in a row—my cycles had always been irregular. My breasts seemed a little bigger, but I thought it was a figment of my imagination. I suppose on some level I'd known. It all made sense. This child growing inside of me was my atonement, and I would spend the rest of my life making things right.

I booked the next flight back to Chicago and then called my mother, telling her that I was coming home. She was waiting for me in international arrivals, right at the gate, her palms clenched together and her face bright.

"Mom," I said, "I made a mistake. A mistake that we'll get to meet in six months."

My mother embraced me, careful not to put pressure on my belly but squeezing tight around my shoulders, telling me she'd never let me leave again. Not without her.

I vowed to make a better life for my daughter; she was my light, my illumination, the source of my hope. I scoured the course catalog of the local community college—ACT scores weren't necessary for admission—and decided on the paralegal program. I thought maybe I could help sexual assault survivors or otherwise be involved with social justice. I also knew that if I worked for a law firm, I might find a kind, bleeding-heart lawyer who valued my intellect and would help me raise my little Cricket.

Remarkably, this plan worked. I met Daniel during my internship at an immigration firm. He was ten years older than me, but I was smart enough not to disclose my age until he'd fallen for me. On our first date, we took a break from writing character reference letters for green-card applicants and had coffee. For our second date, I hired a babysitter, and Daniel took me to a fancy steak house in downtown Chicago. For our third date, we played board games at his lovely Craftsman home, and he talked of introducing me to his parents.

He liked the idea of raising my little Cricket as his own. So much so that he wanted to put his name on her birth certificate and tell her that he was her biological father. I acquiesced. It seemed a small concession for a comfortable life.

And he has provided a good life for us. We want for nothing. Cricket got everything I didn't: swimming and riding lessons, Suzuki method violin, summer camp. Vacations in Colorado and the Caribbean. Sometimes my mother joins us, and she's proved to be an excellent grandmother: patient, loving, and indulgent. And she has kept Cricket's paternity quiet—when Cricket asked about baby photos with Daniel, without missing a beat my mother said they'd been destroyed when our basement flooded. She knows exactly what to reveal and what to keep hidden.

I had mistaken my mother's grief for weakness and favoritism. I was wrong, dead wrong. I can't imagine the depths of pain my mother experienced, because I can't imagine losing Cricket. I'm sad my daughter will never get to meet her uncle Vince.

Now Cricket wants more than Colorado or the Caribbean: she wants Paris. And I don't know that I'm prepared to give it to her.

I think Cricket knows she's wearing me down. My last act of penance is to come clean to my daughter: about her namesake, about her biological father, and about my culpability in this mess. To reveal that she exists because of the actions of a sad, misguided teenage girl. That her mother is no saint.

The choice is relatively simple: I can betray the man I love, or I can betray the love of my life. Daniel will always be her father—it just so happens that they don't share any DNA. As for her sperm donor, I can honestly say I don't know. I suspect it was Anton, but maybe it was Luc. I don't even know their last names.

She and her friend Mikayla are in the den, watching *Amelie* for the fiftieth time and poring over dress catalogs. Cricket has never been particularly girly, but she seems obsessed with finding a dress that suits her personality for the winter formal. She plans to go with a group of her teammates. They've vowed not to shave their legs (the hair creates drag) until regionals. Which are scheduled for a week after the dance.

I bring them popcorn (organic, with some European butter and truffle salt).

"Okay, time-out," I say. "You're at a party and some guy corners you in the bathroom. He may even be your friend—"

Cricket rolls her eyes. "Say I have my period and really bad diarrhea. I know, Mom."

Over the years, Mikayla has been over enough times to understand (and even appreciate) my quirks.

"Is that before or after I kick him in the balls?" Mikayla asks.

"That's up to you. When it happens—I didn't say if—but *when* it happens, you may not be thinking straight. You have to know how to save your*self*."

Suddenly the dress catalog catches my eye. The open page reads "Whitney Ellis" in an elegant serif font. Whitney? I haven't heard from her since I was in Paris, nor have I really wanted to. I've purposefully avoided Facebook and social media—I don't want to be found.

"Whitney Ellis?" I ask. "Is that a designer?"

"Yeah," replies Mikayla. "Her dresses are amazeballs, especially her wedding gowns. My sister wore a Whitney Ellis for her wedding."

Whitney was a famous designer? *Good for her,* I thought. She deserved all the success in the world.

Cricket deserves to know the truth. She's strong enough now to hear it. I book our tickets on Air France and prepare how to tell her. I don't think I'll know until we get up there.

We board the plane. We have seats together on the right-hand side, over the wings. Accustomed to travel, she settles in with her earbuds and iPad, watching a film with Marion Cotillard, her favorite French actress.

My ears still pop on takeoff and landing. I close my eyes. When I open them, I peer through the small window at the blanket of clouds below, amazed just how far I am from earth.

ACKNOWLEDGMENTS

First and foremost, I owe a great debt to my wonderful editor, Carmen Johnson. She always had faith in my abilities, even when I harbored doubt. Carmen recognized the book's raw potential and helped me find the right voice. And my deepest gratitude to agent extraordinaire Julia Kenny, who found the best home for this manuscript.

Many thanks to my literary midwives: Andrea Lochen, Rebecca Adams Wright, and Kristiana Kahakauwila. I'm particularly grateful to Martha Curren-Preis, Ray McDaniel, Sam Scheer, Miriam Lawrence, Kate Middleton, and Meg Levad for their insights and commentary.

And a thank you to my parents for their steadfast love and support.

ABOUT THE AUTHOR

Photo © Dan Lippitt

Kodi Scheer teaches writing at the University of Michigan, where she earned her MFA. She is the author of *Incendiary Girls*.